THE TWO KASHMIRS

AF662744

THE TWO KASHMIRS

A COMPARATIVE ANALYSIS

Sheikh Khalid Jehangir

Vitasta

Published by
Renu Kaul Verma
Vitasta Publishing Pvt Ltd
2/15, Ansari Road, Daryaganj
New Delhi - 110 002
info@vitastapublishing.com

ISBN: 978-93-90961-49-8
© Sheikh Khalid Jehangir
First Edition 2023
MRP ₹ 495

All Rights Reserved.
No part of this publication may be reproduced, stored in a retrieval system, or transmitted in any form, or by any means – electronic, mechanical, photocopying, recording or otherwise – without the prior permission of the publisher.

Typeset & Cover Design by Somesh Kumar Mishra
Printed at Chaman Enterprises, New Delhi

CONTENTS

ACKNOWLEDGEMENTS

The inspiration to write this book comes from my unflinching interest in the politics of Jammu and Kashmir. As a journalist for decades and now as a politician I am on a learning curve constantly reflecting on the nitty gritties of the very nuanced political realities of J&K.

I thank all my friends and colleagues at the ICPS—some of whom were generous with time and effort when they painstakingly read the draft line by line and offered their suggestions as to how to improve the literary and academic quality of the text.

My younger daughter Rania has been unruffled by my frequent cries for help when the computer behaved unpredictably, and she lovingly set it right. She provided me a break by asking innocent questions about the content that I used to think upon.

I would also like to thank my elder daughter Sofia who rendered invaluable assistance by cheerfully typing and proofreading the manuscript. I wish them all the best in their lives.

PREFACE

The Union Territory of Jammu and Kashmir (J&K)[1] in India has suffered the brunt of militancy and terrorism sponsored by Pakistan for more than seven decades. Pakistan's unceasing interference in the affairs of the Indian state has been based on spurious and illegitimate claims and efforts to use force and subversion as tactics to keep J&K permanently volatile and unstable. In 1947, the newly created state of Pakistan, through one of the most brazen acts of invasion and terror, unleashed a horde of marauders (known in history as tribal lashkars) on the unsuspecting people of the erstwhile principality of J&K. These lashkars, enabled by regulars from Pakistan army, let loose a reign of terror and indulged in loot, arson, rape and murder.

1 Until 5 August 2019, the state of J&K included the areas of Jammu, Kashmir and Ladakh.

The ruler of the princely state acceded to India on 27 October 1947, and it was through the efforts of the Indian army, ably assisted by the people of J&K that India managed to repulse the invading force from the valley of Kashmir, but not before they had forcefully occupied a large chunk of the J&K territory, which goes by the name of Pakistan occupied Jammu and Kashmir (PoJK) today. India took the matter to the United Nations (UN) hoping that the international body would take note of Pakistani aggression and direct Pakistan to return the territory illegitimately occupied by it. The efforts of the UN to ascertain the wishes of the people through a plebiscite were not honoured by Pakistan when it refused to reverse the process of aggression and remove its forces as well as Pakistani nationals who had entered the territory under its occupation. The matter was later caught up in the larger cold war geopolitics leading to Indian disenchantment with the process and final approval of accession by the elected representatives from Jammu and Kashmir in 1954. Pakistan continued with its agenda of both subversion or terror and open aggression against India. In July 1972, the two countries signed the famous Simla agreement, whereby Pakistan pledged to settle all matters through 'bilateral' dialogue, implying that the resolutions of the UN were no longer effective for both the countries. In contravention of its own pledge, it has gone ahead with its demand for resolution of the issue through UN resolutions.

It is deplorable that Pakistan continued with its subversion strategy through its use of non-state actors, like it did in 1947, resulting in the perpetuation of violence and terrorism in J&K since 1988-89, causing untold misery and sufferings to the people and unnecessary waste of resources on security to maintain peace and order in J&K. Pakistan has used terror as an instrument of its policy in J&K and used the territory under its illegitimate control as a launching pad to threaten peace and security of India making it difficult for the people of J&K to lead normal lives. It has also affected peace and prosperity of J&K. Through continued propaganda, based on falsehood and misrepresentation of facts, it has tried incessantly to corrupt the minds of the vulnerable youth in J&K and spoil the social and political environment in the J&K, creating the condition for perpetuation of the conflict.

The recent history of J&K shows that Pakistan's continuous interference has also had unprecedented political upheavals in the state. That the princely state of Jammu and Kashmir finally opted to join India, and the people of J&K came down on the streets to cast their lot with Indian army in its efforts to push out the invaders from the valley of Kashmir in 1947-48, did not go down well with Pakistan. The UN sponsored ceasefire in July 1949, led to part of the J&K remaining under Pakistani occupation, which is today known as Pakistan occupied

Jammu Kashmir (PoJK). In March 1963, part of PoJK in the Gilgit-Baltistan area, the Sakhsgam valley, was ceded illegally by Pakistan to China, which along with the Aksai Chin area under illegal control of China, may as well be called China Occupied Kashmir (CoK). However, the present study does not take the CoK area into account and proposes to make a comparative assessment of the situation in J&K and PoJK and brings to fore the socio-political and economic developments in the respective parts of Kashmir.

India has a clearly stated its position on PoJK which India claims is an integral part of it by virtue of the Instrument of Accession as well as the Parliamentary Resolution of 1994. The Survey of India Map shows PoJK and parts of the erstwhile princely state of J&K which are presently under China's control (Aksai Chin and the Trans Karakoram Tract) as an integral part of India. In sync with the official position of India on PoJK, the cartographic representation of these parts is a constant reminder of India's territorial claim on the whole of J&K.

Without any theorization, a comparative analysis of PoJK with that of Jammu and Kashmir has been made in this volume. Based on the findings, it debunks the myth of PoJK being more developed than J&K. This volume brings out facts from credible sources on either side that attest to the fact that J&K is better governed and more developed than PoJK and the situation in J&K could have been much better if Pakistan would not have fuelled terrorism in J&K, especially since the 1990s.

I am extremely grateful to International Centre for Peace Studies and its scholars for collecting necessary data for making this study possible. It is hoped that the present study will add to the existing literature on Jammu and Kashmir and put things in right perspective concerning the Pakistani propaganda about Indian approach to the state affected by cross-border terrorism and conflict.

Sheikh Khalid Jehangir
6 October, 2022
Srinagar

CHAPTER I

The Historical Baggage

THE PRINCELY state of Jammu and Kashmir (J&K) came into existence in the aftermath of the First Anglo-Sikh War (1845-46), following the signing of the Treaty of Amritsar on 16 March 1846. The treaty said that "all the hilly or mountainous country with its dependencies situated to the eastward of the River Indus and the westward of the River Ravi including Chamba and excluding Lahol" would be transferred to the Maharaja of Jammu, "Gulab Singh and heirs male of his body"... "for ever in independent possession." Maharaja Gulab Singh, was made to "pay to the British Government the sum of seventy-five lakhs of rupees (Nanukshahee}" and acknowledge "the supremacy of the British Government" and "in token of such supremacy present annually to the British Government one horse, twelve shawl goats of approved breed (six male and six female) and three pairs of Cashmere shawls." The princely state was now known as Jammu and Kashmir and it consisted of disparate ethnicities, and a multi-regional, multi-faith population under the rule of a Dogra-Rajput dynasty.

The Dogra rulers, through their military prowess and British help, expanded the limits of the J&K State and brought in adjacent areas of Gilgit and Baltistan in the west and northwest, and Kishtwar and Ladakh in east and the northeast into the princely state of J&K. From 1846 till 1947, the princely state was ruled as a single administrative unit. In 1947, the princely state of J&K covered a territory of 2,22,236 sq.kms. After 1947, Pakistan illegally occupied a major chunk of this territory to the east and northwest which has been bifurcated into two different units, i.e., the so-called 'Azad Jammu and Kashmir' ('AJK') which accounts for 13,297 sq. kms. (as per Pakistani figures), and Gilgit-Baltistan (also referred to as Northern Areas after occupation by the government of Pakistan), which accounts for 77,676 sq. kms. (as per Pakistani figures). The Trans Karakoram Tract (Shaksgam Valley) which is part of Gilgit-Baltistan and accounts for 5180 sq. kms. is not included in the 77,676 sq.kms. in the figure shown by Pakistan, and has been ceded to China by Pakistan in 1963 as a result of a provisional Sino-Pak

Border Agreement. The China occupied territory of Kashmir (CoK) in Aksai Chin area accounts for 37,555 sq. kms.[1]

At the time of India's independence, the princely state of J&K was a single administrative unit under Maharaja Hari Singh, the scion of the Dogra dynasty. In April 1935, the British took the Gilgit Agency on a lease for sixty years.[2] However, the lease deed clearly mentioned that "notwithstanding anything in this agreement the said territory shall continue to be included within the dominions of His Highness the Maharaja of Jammu and Kashmir"and the flag of the Kashmir State continued to be flown along with the Union Jack in Gilgit. With the lapse of paramountcy vide 7(l)(b) of the Inidan Independence Act (June-July 1947), "the suzerainty of His Majesty over the Indian States [lapsed]", and with it, "all treaties and agreements in force at the date of the passing of this Act between His Majesty and the rulers of Indian States" also lapsed, whereby the Gilgit Agency, returned to the fold of direct rule by Maharaja. During this period, the rulers of the princely states were theoretically independent, but they were advised to join either of the dominions, because staying independent was not a viable option.

The Indian Independence Act of 1947 had put forth the legal basis for the departure of the British from the subcontinent, and guaranteed partition. To make the transfer of power smooth, a standstill agreement was formulated on 3 June 1947 by the British Indian government, so that all the administrative arrangements that existed between the British crown and the princely state would continue unaltered between the signatory dominions (India and Pakistan) and the state, until new arrangements were made. On 12 August 1947, Jammu and Kashmir sought a standstill agreement with both India and Pakistan, stating, "Jammu and Kashmir government would welcome standstill agreement with Union of India/Pakistan on all matters on which there exists arrangements with the outgoing British India government." India refused to sign the agreement, and asked the Maharaja to send his representative to Delhi for further discussions.

"Government of India would be glad if you or some other minister duly authorized in this behalf could fly to Delhi for negotiating Standstill Agreement between Kashmir Government and India dominion. Early action desirable to maintain intact existing agreements and administrative arrangements," it stated. But no J&K representative visited Delhi for negotiations. However, Pakistan accepted the offer and sent a communication to Jammu and Kashmir Prime Minister Janak Singh on 15 August 1947.

Barely a month later, in a serious breach of the Standstill Agreement, Pakistan not only cut off essential supplies to Jammu and Kashmir, but also hatched a conspiracy with tribal fighters (*lashkars*) to commit aggression on the territory belonging to the princely state under Maharaja in an attempt to acquire it by force. Pakistan hatched a conspiracy with tribal fighters and launched 'Operation Gulmarg' on 22 October 1947 to acquire Jammu and Kashmir by force. As the invaders captured Uri and Baramulla with minimal resistance from the Maharaja's forces, the fall of Srinagar looked imminent. On 24 October, Maharaja Hari Singh appealed to India for military assistance to stop the aggression.

The request was considered on 25 October 1947, in a meeting of India's Defence Committee.[3] In the wake of such unprovoked aggression, the Indian government agreed to offer military assistance to avert the invasion, on the condition that the Instrument of Accession be signed before such help could be extended. The Government of India contended that without a legal sanction, they could not offer military assistance in Maharaja's territory as it would amount to aggression in a neighbouring territory. Hence, the Instrument of Accession was signed with India after due deliberations on 26 October 1947. Post-accession, India was successfully able to contain the Pakistan-led aggression to a large extent. But Pakistan was able to seize a considerable chunk of territory in the western side of the princely state, which is now referred to as the so-called 'Azad Jammu and Kashmir' (AJK) by the Government of Pakistan.

Role of the British in the Rebellion in Gilgit-Baltistan

Another rebellion was underway in the north-eastern J&K known as the Gilgit-Baltistan region, aided by British officers, Major William Alexander Brown and Captain A. S. Mathieson. Brown chose to continue serving the Pakistan army till 1959.[4] The uncertainty regarding the future course of the then princely state of J&K fuelled apprehensions in a section of the local population acting in connivance with the Pakistan army, especially its British officers, who seemed to have understood that the northern frontiers would best serve their strategic purpose if they were under Pakistani control. Fundamentally, the British played an important role in the rebellion. Actually, in the aftermath of World War II, when the British were preparing to transfer power in 1947, they decided to restore the Gilgit Agency[5] (they had taken on lease from the Maharaja in 1935 for sixty years) to the Maharaja thereby abrogating the lease agreement. Having been restored to the Maharaja on 3 June 1947, the the Maharaja sent Brigadier Ghansara Singh as governor to administer this territory.

V.P. Menon writes in *Integration of the Indian States*,

> ....the Maharaja appointed a governor for that area. The governor, accompanied by Major-General H L Scott, chief of staff of the Jammu and Kashmir Army, reached Gilgit on July 30. On arrival, they found that all the officers of the British government had opted

> for service in Pakistan. There was no state civil staff available to take over from these officers. The Gilgit Scouts (raised by the British in 1935) also wanted to go over to Pakistan... At midnight of October 31, [that is, six days after the maharaja signed the instrument of acccssion to India], the governor's residence was surrounded by the Gilgit Scouts. The next morning the governor was put under arrest and a provisional government was established by the rebels. The Muslim elements (including officers) in the state force garrison had deserted; the non-Muslim elements were largely Iiquidated...

The question still remains as to why did Major William Brown, a British officer, join his Muslim colleagues in the Gilgit Scouts in hoisting the Pakistan flag in Gilgit? A plausible explanation is given in a research paper *Three Forgotten Accessions: Gilgit, Hunza and Nagar* by Pakistani scholar Yaqoob Khan Bangash, author of *A Princely Affair: The Accession and Integration of the Princely States of Pakistan, 1947-1955*, and a strong votary of peace and friendship between Pakistan and India. He writes, "By the middle of 1947, news of communal tensions had reached Gilgit and in a place where Hindu Dogras were despised for their heavy-handedness during the conflicts to subdue Gilgit, stories of Muslims being slaughtered by Hindus and Sikhs in the

Punjab inflamed passions against the small minorities of Hindus and Sikhs in Gilgit."

Major Brown was aware of the anti-maharaja sentiments among the people in Gilgit and overassessed the internsity of it. In his subsequent account of the episode, betraying his own sentiments in favour of Pakistan, he wrote in his book *Gilgit Rebellion: The Major Who Mutinied Over Partition of India* :

> ......time had come for me to put my cards on the table. I explained to them that I was just as much in favour of the Province joining Pakistan as they obviously were. I explained to them that in my opinion the only way to prevent a blood bath in Gilgit, such as was taking place downcountry, was for the Province to accede to Pakistan. And I concluded by stating that my immediate intention was to do everything in our power, but with minimum force and bloodshed, to ensure that the Province did become an integral part of Pakistan.....

I shuddered at the thought of the havoc which would follow a decision by the ruler of Kashmir to join India. The blame for the widespread destruction of life and property would lie directly on the British government. I therefore felt it was my duty, as the only Britisher left, to follow a course which would prevent this ... partisan, traitor, revolutionary, I may have been, but that evening my sentiments dictated that if the maharaja acceded to India, then I would forego all allegiance to him and I would not rest content until I had done the utmost in my power to ensure that the Gilgit province joined Pakistan.

The communal, if not pro-Pakistan, sentiment in Gilgit, actively supported by Major Brown put an end to the voices that called for Gilgit's independence from Pakistan, India and the Dogra king. Furthermore, he also prevailed upon the rulers (Mirs) of the two dependencies of the Gilgit Agency, Hunza and Nagar, to join Pakistan in the first week of November 1947. According to a diary entry by George Cunningham, then governor of North-West Frontier Province (NWFP) and one to whom Major Brown reported, the accession of these areas to Pakistan happened without any communal violence and "within two days all the Hindu and Sikh shops were open as usual." The decision of the ruling Mirs of Hunza and Nagar to sign their instruments of accession to Pakistan on November 3 was understandable because "their economies and people were inextricably linked with the Gilgit Agency" whose end signified to them the prospect of living under direct Dogra Raj. "They kept in constant touch with Major Brown in Gilgit and when Major Brown called the Mir of Hunza to confirm if he had earlier in the day on October 30, 1947 affirmed his support for Hari Singh in his accession to India, Hunza clearly came out in favour of Pakistan and said, 'There is only one way for us to go and that is to Pakistan and we shall join Pakistan.'"[6] There is no record of popular resistance to their accession to Pakistan, or of people's demand for accession to India, at the time. However, people in these areas have been agitating against failure of successive Pakistani governments to grant them equal constitutional status.

Thus, Major Brown commanding the Gilgit Scouts[7] volunteered to oversee the region through the process of independence and partition and he staged a coup facilitating Gilgit Baltistan's accession to Pakistan.[8] This is more elaborated by authors in the well researched book *Pakistan Occupied Kashmir: Politics, Parties and Personalities*. They write:

> Major Brown sent frantic wireless messages to Peshawar informing that Pakistan had taken over Gilgit and asked them to send a civil administrator to rule over this region. The Pakistan Government responded by sending Sardar Muhammad Alam, a tehsildar in the North-West Frontier Province (NWFP) government at that time, who assumed the post of Political Agent on November 16, 1947. Because of his strong leaning towards Pakistan, Major Brown played his cards by exploiting the religious sentiments of the Muslims soldiers in Maharaja's army and Gilgit Scouts to incite them to revolt and detach Northern Areas from rest of Kashmir.[9]

Many British officers in the region had opted to serve in Pakistan. They were able to manipulate the situation to their advantage. They successfully played the 'divide and rule' card to urge the Muslim officers and soldiers in the J&K state army to desert ranks and join the rebellion. These deserters and the Gilgit Scouts marched towards Gilgit and took the governor into captivity. The British deemed it appropriate that the strategic Northern Frontier should remain with Pakistan who they believed would be more amenable to their future strategic pulls and pressures. Having taken control of Gilgit, the Pakistani forces moved to seize the adjoining areas such as the Burzila pass, Gurais (also written as Gurez), and Skardu in Baltistan that stretch till Kargil. These forces were able to hold key positions in the region before the onset of winter, when these areas become inaccessible. Indian troops, therefore, could not counter these forces for the next few months.[10]

The flag of Pakistan was hoisted by William Brown on 1 November 1947. A revolutionary interim self-government was constituted in Gilgit under Raja Shah Rais Khan but it lasted only for 16 days. It is believed that the provisional government did not sign a formal Instrument of Accession with Pakistan. Instead, a wireless message was sent to the government of Pakistan to send a civil administrator.[11] Thereafter, Sardar Muhammad

Alam was sent on 16 November 1947. It is argued that the common people of Gilgit-Baltistan had not participated in the rebellion.[12] The British calculations were largely based on the assumption that in a region where the majority of the population was Muslim, the popular desire would be to align with Pakistan. However, in reality in some of the Muslim majority areas in J&K, for example in Gurez, Tithwal and Keran, the local populace, worried about the invasion by tribal lashkars, actually sent their representatives to Srinagar to push back the invaders and many of these areas still remain on the Indian side of the earlier Ceasefire Line drawn up in 1949, and the Line of Control (LoC), which was drawn up in 1972.

For a short period, the Gilgit-Baltistan region was administered by the 'AJK' government, prior to the signing of the Karachi Agreement in April 1949 that abrogated AJK's authority over the area. It was governed through the Frontier Crimes Regulations (FCR), which also applied to tribal areas of Pakistan. Under FCR, people had no right to appeal, to legal representation or to present reasoned evidence. With the passage of time, there was an increasing realization among the people in Gilgit-Baltistan that it had been a mistake on their part to remain silent about the process that unfolded in 1947 to bring the region under Pakistani occupation. The growing discontent was evident in the political movements that emerged as early as 1957. The Gilgit League was formed to oppose the FCR and to demand basic political and democratic rights for the people of Gilgit-Baltistan. More nationalist groups like the Tanzeem-e-Millat and Gilgit-Baltistan Jamhoori Mahaz were formed in the later years to create awareness regarding basic political and constitutional rights among the people of Gilgit-Baltistan.[13]

Acession with India and its Aftermath

The Maharaja of Kashmir signed the Instrument of Accession in India's favour on 26 October 1947. This accession applied to Gilgit-Baltistan (GB) as well because it was very much a part of J&K. Therefore, both GB and the so called 'AJK' are historically and legitimately a part of India. In the years following independence and partition, the issue of Kashmir acquired prominence on the world stage. It got embroiled in the Cold War dynamics and India's non-aligned position was regarded unfavourably by the US and Western countries. The focus, thus, remained on the J&K on the Indian side while the area illegally occupied by Pakistan during theh tribal invasion,[14] which was the main reason for break out of violence in October 1947 and brought the two countries to war, was clearly overlooked and forgotten over time. This unaddressed and fully-unrepulsed invasion has resulted in India losing substantial chunk of territory in western Kashmir, which is termed PoJK including the 'AJK' and GB. Since, Pakistan continues to hold the territory of 'AJK' illegally, it has been a major stumbling block on the path of materialization of peace in the state of Jammu and Kashmir. Pakistan has, ever since, collaborated with a menagerie of non-state actors to challenge the might of the Indian state in Kashmir resulting in hundreds of thousands of security forces being deployed in Kashmir. Sponsoring terrorism in Kashmir has been an instrument of its policy to weaken India and pose a critical security challenge to India. An important component of this sub-conventional strategy has been to poison the minds of the people of Jammu and Kashmir through unremitting anti-India propaganda, riding on allegations of mis-governance and nepotical rule in J&K by puppet regimes of New Delhi in the state. In reality, the curious case of granting of a special status courtesy Article 370 of the Indian Constitution had insulated local representative government from New Delhi's intervention. This insulation had empowered a crop of self-seeking political leaders who took full advantage of the 'special status' to perpetuate their hold on power and exploit the sentiments of people, often using the false narrative spawned by Pakistan. The deep state of Pakistan continues to use militant proxies for securing its two vital objectives; first, its key strategic interests in both India and Afghanistan and second; keep Kashmir on the boil for ever. Within India, the proxies have been employed to hurt Indian interests and bringing peace to the valley of Kashmir, whereas, in Afghanistan, they are engaged to ensure that the country remains within Pakistan's control and does not become a secure base for India.[15]

The forced annexation of Gilgit-Baltistan by Pakistan, was thus overlooked because of:

- Pakistan's loud and irrational claims over J&K,
- the outbreak of violence and
- the partisan role played by the international community and organizations.

Gilgit and Baltistan along with Hunza, Nagar part of the erstwhile Ladakh Wazarat were amalgamated in 1970.[16] Later, the FCR was abolished by former Prime Minister, Zulfiqar Ali Bhutto in 1974 and certain administrative and judicial reforms were introduced to defuse the situation. The process of reforms ended abruptly when Zia-ul-Haq came to power and imposed martial law in 1977 in Pakistan. In 1982, General Zia-ul-Haq made a failed attempt to effect some reforms by taking select members of the Northern Areas (or GB) Council to the Majlis-e-Shura. He abandoned the move in the face of strong protests from the 'AJK' Kashmiris who believed the Northern Areas were not a part of Pakistan. There were reports of protests from India too. When Benazir Bhutto came to power in the late 1980s, she resumed the process of reform and although most of them were inconsequential, they led to the first ever party-based elections in Gilgit-Baltistan in October 1994.

Gilgit-Baltistan region, as has been discussed earlier, was commonly termed as the strategic northern frontiers facing Britain's arch imperial rival, Russia during the colonial period. Precisely for this strategic value, the region was kept under British lease since 1935, for a period of 60 years. The lease was terminated in view of British withdrawal, and hence, the control of the region was restored to the Maharaja of Kashmir.

There is a view that during the time the region was under the suzerainty of Maharaja of Kashmir, after the British restored it to the Maharaja, there was a window of opportunity for him to declare local autonomy within the state of J&K. Such a pre-emptive measure could have pacified the brewing unrest amongst particular sections of the population and averted the crisis, which eventually occurred. Unfortunately, this did not happen in the frenzy of celebrations as the region reverted to rule by Maharaja of Kashmir. On his visit to Srinagar in the beginning of August 1947, Mahatma Gandhi foresaw "the seeds of future trouble in an unqualified inclusion of Gilgit in Kashmir." Mahatma Gandhi's thinking predicted the impending trouble. The newly appointed Governor, Brigadier Ghansara Singh, the Maharaja's representative, was captured by rebels who declared the region's accession to Pakistan by hoisting a Pakistani flag in Gilgit.

This historical account provides an overview of the way the 'other Kashmir' or PoJK came under Pakistan's illegal control to begin with and how the British officers as well as the international community contributed to such an illegal takeover in the post-partition period. It is ironical that the so called free-world led by the US failed to support the secular, liberal and democratic values that dictated India's policies and backed the logic of partition that led to emphasis on communal politics. They were consumed by the argument that as a Muslim majority state, J&K should have logically joined Pakistan, little realising that the leaders of India rejected such idea, even when they agreed to partition to avert a communal crisis. It is also conveniently forgotten that during the tribal lashkar invasion, the people of Kashmir stood solidly behind the Indian efforts during 1947-48 and fearing overwhelming popular support for India, the Pakistani leadership refused to honour the UN resolution for a plebiscite in 1948.

In the succeeding days, India went further and incoroporated an exceptional provision in its Constitution in the shape of Article 370 to grant the people of J&K autonomy of a kind not envisioned in any developed democracies of the time. However, it is interesting that such provisions created the condition for the rise of an irresponsive and self-seeking leadership that took full advantage of Pakistan sponsored militancy/terrorism and disregarded popular aspirations for development and peace. In fact, a separatist leadership emerged in the horizon supported by Pakistan and was treated rather generously and kind-heartedly by the Indian state. All this throttled the process of representative politics and created a culture of corruption, nepotism and violence, which persisted for along time, until the Indian government took a decision to abrogate Article 370 and better integrate the erstwhile state with India.

It is interesting to note that despite Pakistan's bid to arrest the process of democratic politics and interrupt the course of development in J&K, the indices of growth and development in J&K are in clear contrast to the indices on the other side of the LoC in PoJK. Were it not for Pakistan's constant meddling in J&K, the state would have attained peace and prosperity to a degree that would have inspired the envy of other states in India.

End Notes

1 If we leave out the territories illegally occupied by Pakistan and China, the area left with India accounts for 93,708 sq. kms. However, going by official figures in India, the total area with India is 1,01,387 sq. kms.

2 A lease deed was signed on 26 March 1935 bearing the signatures of Maharaja Hari Singh and British Resident in Kashmir, L. E. Lang. It was ratified by the Viceroy Lord Wellington on 3 April 1935.

3 For more, see, Shabir Choudhry, *Tribal Invasion and Kashmir: Pakistani Attempts to Capture Kashmir in 1947, Division of Kashmir and Terrorism*, Bloomington: Author House, 2013, p. 17.

4 Surinder Kumar Sharma, Yaqoob ul Hassan and Ashok Behuria, *Pakistan Occupied Kashmir: Politics, Parties and Personalities*, Pentagon Press LLP, New Delhi, 2019.

5 The agency consisted of Gilgit, as well as subsidiary principalities of Chilas, Darel and Tangir, Koh-Ghizr, Yasin, Ishkoman, Punial, Hunza and Nagar. For a detailed account of the Gilgit Agency see Amar Singh Chohan, *Gilgit Agency 1877–1935*, Atlantic Publishers, New Delhi, 1997.

6 For more, see, Sudheendra Kulkarni, "How and Why Gilgit Baltistan Defied Maharaja Hari Singh and Joined Pakistan", *The Wire*, 2020, accessed June 30, 2022, at URL: https://thewire.in/diplomacy/how-and-why-gilgit-baltistan-defied-maharaja-hari-singh-and-joined-pakistan

7 Ibid,

8 Surinder Kumar Sharma, Yaqoob ul Hassan and Ashok Behuria, *Pakistan Occupied Kashmir: Politics, Parties and Personalities*, Pentagon Press LLP, New Delhi, 2019.

9 Ibid, p. 125.

10 Bal Raj Madhok, *Kashmir: The Centre of the World Storm,* accessed July 30, 2022, at URL: https://archive.org/details/MergedF681b8be4cc54471BfcfD2d477673ef0/page/n2/mode/2up

11 Ahmad Hasan Dani, *History of the Northern Areas of Pakistan*, p. 349.

12 Subroto Roy, *Pakistan's Allies*, June 5, 2006.

13 Altaf Hussain, *The Gilgit Baltistan Reforms 2009*, Report by the Forum of Federations Project, December 2009.

14 Christopher Snedden's book *Understanding Kashmir and Kashmiris* goes against the popular narrative that the tribal invasion was the first instance of violence in J&K. Instead, he argues, much before Pakhtoon tribesman invaded Kashmir in October 1947, there was rebellion in Poonch, 'Azad Kashmir' and Gilgit and Baltistan against the Maharaja. The importance that Snedden gives to the communal violence in Jammu – he even blames the tribal invasion by Pashtun tribesmen backed by the Pakistan army on the Jammu violence and presents it as the catalyst for the eventual Partition of the state of Jammu and Kashmir – flies in the face of historical facts. There is enough evidence available that the planning for the tribal invasion had commenced months before the Jammu communal violence. Snedden himself accepts this when he points out that Pandit Nehru had informed Sardar Patel about the shenanigans of the NWFP and Punjab governments in the newly created Pakistan to stir trouble in J&K.

15 C. Christine Fair, *In Their Own Words: Understanding Lashkar-e-Tayyaba*, Oxford University Press, New Delhi, 2019, p. 10.

16 For a comprehensive Pakistani perspective on Gilgit Baltistan's history, see, Ahmad Hasan Dani, *History of the Northern Areas of Pakistan*, Sang-e-Meel Publications, Karachi, 2001.

CHAPTER II

Demographic Profile of J&K and PoJK

THE DEVELOPMENTAL scenario of any state is positively correlated to its demographic profile, which affects its socio-economic indicators. The population statistics include population size, sex ratio, density and dependency ratio, while vital statistics include indicators such as birth rate, death rate, natural growth rate, life expectancy at birth, mortality and fertility rates. It, thereby, provides an overview of population size, composition, territorial distribution, changes therein and the components of changes such as natality, mortality, and social mobility.

This section provides an overview of the salient

demographic characteristics of J&K and PoJK so as to contextualise the comparative analysis of their different socio-economic indicators ahead. The last census in Jammu and Kashmir was conducted in 2011, whereas in PoJK, it was in 2017. However, for the sake of uniformity, the study relies on the population estimates provided by the respective governments in these two regions as of 2020-21.

Population

In terms of population, the Government of India Census of 2011 recorded the population of J&K at 12.51 million, constituting 6.6 million males and 5.9 million females. As of 2021, the population, taking into consideration its decadal growth rate, is estimated at 13,635,010, including 7.2 million males and 6.4 million females. On the other hand, the population of PoJK, including Gilgit-Baltistan (GB), according to the 2017 Census, was recorded at 5.53 million, including 2.75 million males and 2.78 million females. As of 2020, the population of PoJK is estimated to be 5.73 million, which includes 2.84 million males and 2.89 million females.

The population density of J&K is 132 people per sq. kms., whereas it is 66 people per sq. kms. in PoJK. In terms of urbanisation in these two regions, the percentage of J&K's urban population is around 27.38 per cent, which is more than PoJK's 22.53 per cent.

Table 1.1: Geographical Area and Population of PoJK and J&K

Indicator	J&K	PoJK
Area (sq. kms.)	101,387	83,294
Population Size (projected)	13,635,010	5,525,287
Population (Male)	7,217,010	2,844,070
Population (Female)	6,423,000	2,893,432
Population density (per sq. km.)	132	66
Urban Population percentage	27.38	22.53
Sex Ratio	889 (2011)	1042 (2017)
Birth Rate (per 1000)	15.4	46.9
Mortality Rate (per 1000)	4.9	NA

Source: For J&K the source of the data is J&K official government website. For PoJK the sources of data for both 'AJK' and 'GB' are respective government websites.[1]

The Sex Ratio of PoJK is in favour of females and comparatively better than J&K. For every 1000 males in PoJK, there are 1042 females. In the case of J&K, the sex ratio as per the 2011 census was recorded at 889, which is expected to improve marginally, given the improvement in sex ratio at birth to 946 by 2020. The Birth Rate in J&K is 15.4 per 1000, whereas there is no data available for 'AJK' and for Gilgit-Baltistan, it is 46.9 per 1000. The life expectancy (at birth) in J&K is 72.2 years, whereas the same for 'AJK' and GB in PoJK are 67.3 years and 68.1 years, respectively, thereby signifying a better score for J&K.

Total Fertility Rate (TFR), which is one of the important indicators in the demographic profile of any state, is significantly less for J&K with 2.02 children per woman, as against 3.5 children per woman and 4.7 children per woman for PoJK's two administrative regions of 'AJK' and GB respectively.

In terms of the average household size, the average household in J&K comprises 5.92 people per household, whereas it is 6.7 people per household in 'AJK' and 8.99 people per household in GB of PoJK respectively.

Table 1.2 Average Household Size in PoJK and J&K

Indicator	J&K	PoJK	
		'AJK'	GB
Average Household size (people per household)	5.92	6.7	8.99
Life Expectancy at Birth (years)	72.2	67.3	68.1
Fertility Rate (children per woman)	2.02	3.5	4.7

Source: The date for both J&K and PoJK ('AJK' & 'GB') is from their respective government websites.[2]

Literacy

Literacy, defined as the ability to read and write with understanding, reflects the socio-economic and cultural milieu of a nation, ethnic group or community. J&K and 'AJK' part of PoJK are evenly placed in literacy rates, with 77.30 per cent and 77.50 per cent respectively. However, Gilgit-Baltistan fares abysmally with just a 53 per cent literacy rate, with women at 41 per cent. This manifests Pakistan's continued discrimination against the occupied region, given its marginal progress in two decades from when the literacy in GB was recorded at 38 per cent in 1998. The literacy rates of the J&K and PoJK are tabulated as:

Table 1.3: Literacy Rate of PoJK and J&K

Indicator	J&K	PoJK	
		'AJK'	GB
Literacy Rate percentage	77.30	77.5	53
Male percentage	85.70	87.8	66
Female percentage	68	67.7	41

Source: The date for both J&K and POJK ('AJK' & 'GB') is from their respective government websites.[3]

Religious Composition

J&K, a Muslim majority (68.31 per cent) region in India, presents a pluralistic character with a substantial Hindu population (28.44 per cent), apart from other religious denominations. J&K has maintained this diverse religious base since the partition of British India into India and Pakistan in 1947, which is not the case with PoJK, which saw the proportion of the Hindu population receding to insignificant numbers. The religious composition of J&K and PoJK is given below:

Table 1.4 Religious Composition in J&K and PoJK		
Religion	**J&K**	**PoJK**
Muslims percentage	68.31	99.8
Hindus percentage	28.44	Na
Sikhs percentage	1.87	Na
Buddhists percentage	0.90	Na
Christians percentage	0.28	Na
Others percentage	0.20	0.2

Source: The date for both J&K and POJK ('AJK' & 'GB') is from their respective government websites.[4]

Ethnic groups and Languages

J&K is a heterogeneous state and is home to diverse ethnic groups. Every region of the state possesses different ethnic backgrounds, professing diverse religions, cultures and languages. The major ethnic groups living in J&K include Kashmiris, Gujjars, Bakarwals, Paharis, Dogras and Ladakhis. The principal spoken languages of the state are Kashmiri, Urdu, Dogri, Gojri, Pahari, Hindi, Balti, Pashto and Punjabi.

The population of PoJK also consists of many diverse linguistic and ethnic groups, like Gujjars, Sudhans, Awans, Mughals, Jats, Rajputs, and Kashmiris in the 'AJK' region and Shinas, Yashkuns, Kashmiris, Kashgaris, Pamiris, Pathans, and Kohistanis in the GB region. Kashmiris in 'AJK' are majorly concentrated in and around Neelam Valley and Leepa Valley. The principal languages in PoJK are Pahari-Pothwari, Gojri, Kashmiri,

Shina, Balti, Burushaski, Khowar and Wakhi, with Urdu being the official language and lingua franca across both sides of the Line of Control.

Issues concerning the children

J&K has comparatively better indicators when it comes to the issues concerning the children. The state Infant Mortality Rate (IMR) per 1000 live births stands at 32.4, which is significantly better than that of 'AJK'at 47 and GB at 71.4 in the Pakistani-occupied territory of J&K. In the case of the Percentage of stunted children, J&K scores 27.2 per cent against 39.3 per cent of 'AJK'and 46.6 per cent of GB. Likewise, in the case of the percentage of wasted children, J&K measures 12.7 per cent against the 16.1 per cent of 'AJK' in PoJK. Interestingly, the data shows GB fares marginally better at 9.4 per cent. Further, in the case of the percentage of underweight children, J&K recorded 18 per cent against PoJK's average of 21.6 per cent.

Table 1.5 Issues concerning Children of J&K and PoJK

Indicator	J&K	PoJK	
		'AJK'	GB
Infant mortality rate (per 1000 live births)	32.4	47	71.4
Percentage stunted children	27.7	39.3	46.6
Percentage wasted children	12.7	16.1	9.4
Percentage underweight children	18	21.9	21.3
Percentage overweight children	6.50	12.2	13.4

Source: The date for both J&K and POJK ('AJK' & 'GB') is from their respective government websites.[5]

Asset Ownership

In the case of asset ownership across the Line of Control, the percentage of households owning a TV in J&K is 71.5 per cent, against 69.0 per cent for 'AJK' and 57.8 per cent for GB. For the households owning a refrigerator, 'AJK' is better placed with 61.1 per cent against 47.2 per cent of J&K. In GB, it is 27.1 per cent, which is significantly low.

Table 1.6 Asset Ownership in J&K and PoJK

Indicator	J&K	PoJK	
		'AJK'	GB
Percentage of households with a TV	71.5	69.0	57.8
Percentage of households with a refrigerator	47.2	61.1	27.1
Percentage of households with a washing machine	35.4	60.2	38.4
Percentage of households with a motorbike	23.2	32.8	27.9
Percentage of households with a computer	11.9	17.7	21.9

Source: The date for both J&K and POJK ('AJK' & 'GB') is from their respective government websites.[6]

The demographic profiles of both parts of J&K show that in terms of asset ownership, infant mortality, literacy rate, infant mortality, infant health, life expectancy etc. J&K has much better figures than PoJK. As has been pointed out above, this is despite the fact that J&K has been the target of Pakistan-sponsored terrorism since the late 1980s.

End Notes

1 For J&K refer to https://jk.gov.in/, for 'AJK' refer to https://www.ajk.gov.pk/, and for 'GB' refer to https://www.cmgb.gov.pk/
2 Ibid.
3 Ibid.
4 Ibid.
5 Ibid.
6 Ibid.

CHAPTER III

Evolution of Politics in PoJK and J&K

THE PRINCELY state of J&K lost parts of its territory, both in the west and north-west illegally occupied by Pakistan and in the east illegally occupied by China. In the north, the trans-Karakoram tract in the Shakshgam valley—a tract of 5,180 sq. kms. was ceded to China by Pakistan in 1963, as a gesture to cement then evolving Sino-Pakistan strategic alliance. Henceforth, Pakistan occupied Kashmir (PoK), also known as Pakistan occupied Jammu and Kashmir (PoJK) refers to both the parts of the erstwhile princely state of J&K consisting of the so-called Azad Jammu and Kashmir (AJK) and Gilgit-Baltistan (GB).[1] Today, they are separate administrative units even though they share a common origin.

Azad by Name Alone History and Politics

Pakistan Occupied Jammu and Kashmir (PoJK) remains in a state of uncertainty ever since it was illegally brought under the control of Pakistani security forces in October 1947. On April 28, 1949, Pakistan bifurcated the territory under its occupation into two separate political entities. One of these, more populous but consisting of about 15 per cent of the occupied territory, was called 'Azad Jammu and Kashmir' ('AJK'), and given the notional status of an 'Azad' or independent state but in reality, it was administered de facto by a minister in charge of Kashmir and Northern Areas (KANA) in Islamabad till 1974, and by an executive council headed by Prime Minister of Pakistan.[2] The history of Pakistan's dealings with 'AJK' reveal that it is not even autonomous, let alone 'Azad' (translated as independence or freedom in English), by any stretch of imagination. As elucidated by one observer from the area:

> One can vaguely deduce the status of 'AJK' from the statement that Azad Kashmir is neither a sovereign state nor a province of Pakistan but rather a 'local authority' with responsibility over the areas assigned to it under the ceasefire agreement.[3]

The ceasefire agreement was signed between the military representatives of India and Pakistan on July 27, 1949. After the ceasefire agreement, Pakistan, quite smartly, demobilised the so called 'Azad Kashmir' soldiers by applying the Pakistan Army Act over 'AJK,' which was notionally 'independent.' Thus, Pakistan succeeded in controlling the occupied part of Jammu and Kashmir without any resistance. Initially, the 'AJK' government, under Sardar Muhammad Ibrahim, whom Pakistan installed as the first President, tried to be assertive in demanding recognition of the 'Provisional "Azad" Government' from Pakistan and the United Nations Commission for India and Pakistan (UNCIP) officials.[4] But this assertiveness was short-lived. Neither the UNCIP, nor Pakistan was interested in recognising the 'Provisional "Azad" Government' as a legitimate and independent government. The 'AJK' government was soon reduced to the position of a mere municipal authority without any substantial power. Instead, all power was vested in a ministry called Ministry of Kashmir Affairs (MKA)—later, it became Ministry of Kashmir and Northern Affairs (KANA)—in Islamabad, to rule over the occupied territory. There was an opening for the 'AJK' government to raise its voice independently in any forum. Mushtaq Ahmad Gurmani, who signed on the Karachi Agreement of April 1949 as a minister without portfolio, was made the first to head the MKA. His shrewd politics of divide and rule helped him establish strong control over the affairs of 'AJK.'[5] By driving a wedge between the Muslim Conference President, Chaudhary Ghulam Abbas, and

Sardar Ibrahim, the President of 'AJK,' he ensured his tight hold over 'AJK.' While analysing the role played by the MKA in imposing Pakistan's writ on the region, Snedden sums up:

> MKA manipulation meant that it went 'without saying' that no Azad Kashmir president could 'sanely, think of keeping himself in [the] saddle if and when the Government of Pakistan wants him to quit.' They stayed in office, or left, on MKA orders. This Pakistani bureaucrat and his colleagues ensured that Pakistan's writ applied throughout Azad Kashmir. They also treated the Azad Kashmir president and senior Azad Kashmir Government officials as second-class citizens. It was 'quite normal' that Azad Kashmir 'chief executives' should wait outside the office of the joint secretary, who theoretically was subordinate to the Azad Kashmiris, before they were 'called in' at his pleasure. Azad Kashmiris had to accept such belittling treatment. Their region lacked international recognition and it was dependent on Pakistan for many things, including financial, military and physical support, such as food grains and basic staples.[6]

According to the terms of the 1949 Karachi Agreement, the 'AJK' government became an adjunct of the Pakistan state. The agreement divided the functions among the three signatories – the Government of Pakistan, Azad

Kashmir Government, and Muslim Conference. This agreement defined 'AJKs' relationship with Pakistan. The leaders of Muslim Conference were made to lose their control over Gilgit and Ladakh areas as mentioned in the agreement, which was to be administered by a political agent to be appointed by the government of Pakistan. In the very beginning, instead of giving importance to representative government or democracy, priority was given to raising an army. But soon after that Islamabad felt compelled to form a government in order to run the day-to-day affairs of the land occupied after the July 1949 ceasefire agreement with India.

The Karachi agreement of 28 April 1949 was, to a large extent, modelled after the Rules of Business enunciated to run the affairs of the provisional Azad Kashmir government. It was formed with Pakistani blessings on 24 October 1947, sans legal and constitutional framework. This government declared itself as a 'War Council' with the single objective of 'liberating' the parts of J&K which remained under Indian control.[7] This War Council had formalised the Rules of Business for running the administration of the region. The President was vested with both executive and legislative powers, and nominated under the Rules of Business by the pleasure of the General Council of the Muslim Conference. But both were under the control of the Chief Advisor appointed by the Government of Pakistan.[8] To run the judicial system, courts were created and laws codified, "some laws of Punjab were adopted for the state while a good body of the former Jammu and Kashmir State Code was retained.[9]

But things went wrong with the release of Chaudhary Ghulam Abbas (4 February, 1904–18 December, 1967) in March 1948 by Sheikh Abdullah who became the Chief Emergency Administrator after the Maharaja acceded to India and agreed to put in place a popular administrative machinery in the state. Abbas became the supreme head of the Muslim Conference in 1949.[10] The Working Committee of the Muslim Conference adopted a resolution on 2 March 1949 to give significant powers to the supreme head. These powers included appointment of the President and other members of the council. The Government of Pakistan did not show any hesitation in recognising the supremacy of Ghulam Abbas. Rather they found it easier to do business with Abbas than with Sardar Ibrahim. Very soon, there was a clash of personality; Abbas and Ibrahim fell out with each other. They discovered that they differed in their political beliefs. Abbas not only dismissed Ibrahim's government in 1950 but was also vehemently opposed against any democratic set-up in the region. According to Ershad Mahmud,

> "He was not in favour of establishing a democratic set-up as he thought that electoral politics would take

> leaders, parties and the people away from the cause of liberation. Above all, the 'AJK' politics revolved around the clan system, and Chaudhary Abbas, being from the other side of the J&K state, had no roots in the area."[11]

Three distinguished personalities started controlling the politics of 'AJK.' There were three different Muslim Conferences fighting among themselves for influence, led by Ghulam Abbas, Sardar Ibrahim and Mirwaiz Yusuf Shah who was from an influential religious family in Srinagar and uncle of Mirwaiz Umar Farooq of Srinagar and leader of his faction of Hurriyat Conference in the valley today.

Taking advantage of this struggle for power in 'AJK,' among different personalised factions of Muslim Conference, the Rules of Business were revised in 1952, and instead of aiming at creating a balance of power between the 'AJK' government and the Muslim Conference and empowering the people to elect their leader, the new Rules vested all powers with the MKA.[12] Now the President was elected according to the wishes of the MKA. The revisions weakened the grip of the Muslim Conference on state affairs. It was signed by the President, Colonel Sher Ahmad Khan, who hailed from Sudhan Biradari—a powerful tribe in 'AJK'—and was politically inept. The new Rules reduced Azad Kashmir to the stature of a municipality. The MKA not only abolished the office of the Supreme Head (read President of the Muslim Conference), but under the rules, it was to be consulted on almost all matters undertaken by the Azad Kashmir Government. It also had supervisory power over the executive. The MKA was thus vested with supreme legal authority to deal with the affairs of Azad Kashmir and a Joint Secretary in the Ministry wielded disproportionate power. Snedden writes that "four years after being a belligerent anti-Indian fighting force, the Azad Kashmir movement was emasculated. It now was a supplicant, not a surrogate."[13]

The Rules of Business were revised again for the third time in 1958. Under the new Rules, a Chief Advisor was introduced who replaced the Joint Secretary. Ironically, the Chief Advisor was to be selected by the Minister in charge of Kashmir Affairs (MKA), not by the Government of Azad Kashmir. This Ministry later changed its name to Ministry of Kashmir Affairs and Northern Areas (MKANA). After the revisions in 1958, all functions of the 'AJK' government were exercised in the name of the president, while real power was exercised by MKANA officials. The 'AJK' government was not even allowed to create any post which had a monthly salary of over Rs. 150, and was not allowed to spend over Rs. 100,000 without the permission of MKANA. Thus, the Pakistani Government, through various institutions and constitutional acts, not only strengthened its hands at the cost of the 'AJK' government, but also ensured that it was in full control of 'AJKs' internal political affairs. Successive governments in 'AJK' were removed and appointed at will on the whims of the government in Islamabad. During 1947-1959, over a period of 12 years, there were eight presidents (one of them was selected twice). The Pakistani state's suspicion regarding the political agenda of Azad Jammu and Kashmir Muslim Conference (AJKMC), often led to such frequent change of leadership in 'AJK.' Under the presidential system, during 1958-1970, the political and administrative rights granted to the 'AJK' Government were minimal.

After taking over power in Pakistan in October 1958 in a bloodless coup, General Ayub Khan introduced 'Basic Democracy' on the basis of party-less elections. He banned all political parties and activities in Pakistan. Initially, Ayub did not introduce 'Basic Democracy' in 'AJK,' and appointed K.H. Khurshid, one time private secretary to Muhammad Ali Jinnah, as the President of 'AJK' on May 1, 1959. Ayub Khan held elections in 'AJK' in 1961. Khurshid won the elections to become the first elected president and later formed a party called Jammu and Kashmir Liberation League (JKLL) because of his differences with AJKMC. He remained in that post till 1964, when he developed differences with the establishment and had to quit.

Right from the beginning of his tenure, Khurshid was not well received by the MKA. He was branded as uncooperative and difficult to work with. Moreover, his strained relationship with AJKMC leadership, particularly with Chaudhary Ghulam Abbas, was also another issue that led to a power struggle, in which Khurshid's opponents – the MKA and AJKMC– got the better of him and the news of his resignation, 'on personal grounds' was announced by the government in Islamabad on August 5, 1964. Some accounts say that a mid-level police official forced him to resign and months later he was kept in detention in Palandari and Dalai camp for some months. What hastened his removal was a strong rumour in Pakistan that he had warmed up to Sheikh Abdullah during the latter's trip (May 24-27, 1964) to 'AJK' and was planning for an independent Kashmir.

After his resignation, Khurshid struggled to keep himself and his party politically relevant, but without much success. Later, he died a pauper in a road accident on March 11, 1988, while travelling in a public transport vehicle with Rs 37/- in his pocket (Dawn, March 11, 2011). Ironically, Khurshid was appointed President of 'AJK' by the military and was also removed by it when he sought to move towards independence from Pakistan's control. Khurshid was replaced by Khan Abdul Hamid Khan, former Chief Justice of 'AJK' High Court, and brother of Sardar Qayyum Khan who had become

President of 'AJK' for less than a year from September 8, 1956 – April 13, 1957. Abdul Hamid Khan remained president for more than five years allowing himself to be brazenly guided and controlled by the Pakistan government and security forces. Like Khurshid, he ruled without any cabinct and tried to consolidate his position in 'AJK.'[14]

The period following Khurshid's ouster witnessed continued marginalizsation of the people, which led to a wave of agitations launched by leading 'AJK' based political parties against the MKA. Sardar Ibrahim, and Sardar Muhammad Abdul Qayyum Khan, the successor of Ghulam Abbas, joined hands to weaken the MKA's control over 'AJK.' They demanded elected and responsible government—an elected president and a legislature with full powers of legislation, including the budget approving power.

When Ayub's regime was replaced by Gen. Yahya Khan in March 1969, 'AJK' was given some nominal degree of political autonomy. Yahya Khan appointed a retired army general, Abdul Rahman Khan, his own man, as the minister of the MKA. After consulting all the stakeholders of 'AJK,' he announced that democratic rule would be introduced soon in the region. Finally, a democratic set-up was introduced in 'AJK' through the 1970 Act. Under this Act, adult franchise was introduced in 'AJK' and the President of 'AJK' was to be elected on the basis of one person-one vote. Apart from adult electorates from 'AJK', the refugees from Jammu and Kashmir settled in other areas of Pakistan were also eligible to cast their votes.

The 1970 Act introduced a directly elected 'AJK' Assembly with 24 elected members and one nominated lady member. The assembly was granted some legislative powers while defence, foreign affairs and currency remained the preserve of the government of Pakistan. It even had the power to remove the president by two-third majority. The state subject law—that bars non-Kashmiris from getting state citizenship—also became part of this act in deference to local opinion.

After 1970s, Pakistan broke up into East and West Pakistan and East Pakistan paved a way to today's Bangladesh. The outcome of the 1971 War, although it was not fought over the issue of Kashmir, affected the politics of the region in a significant manner. The following factors played an important role in 'AJK' politics after 1971:

(i) There was a growing demand in 'AJK' for a parliamentary system of government from the local chapter of Pakistan Peoples' Party (PPP) when Zulfiqar Bhutto got a new constitution drafted which put in place a parliamentary form of government in Pakistan. The local chapter of PPP Azad Kashmir (AJKPPP) lobbied Bhutto for a similar system in 'AJK.' Therefore, presidential system of government, which had worked for about 4 years, was replaced by a parliamentary system introduced under the "AJK interim Constitution Act, 1974." This so called 'Interim' act has had a long run for more than four decades and undergone about 13 amendments till 2018. The Assembly consisted of 40 members, elected on the basis of adult franchise and two co-opted lady members. Today, the Assembly consists of 41 elected Members (29 from 'AJK' proper and 12 from among the refugees) and 8 co-opted members – 5 women, one member *from Ullema-e- Din/Mushaikh*, one from among the 'AJK' technocrats and other professionals, and one from amongst 'AJK' nationals residing abroad.

(ii) According to many scholars, Zulfiqar Bhutto and then Prime Minister of India, Indira Gandhi, had reached an understanding about settling the issue around the status quo recognising the Line of Control (LoC) as the international border. Under the Simla Agreement in 1972, both sides decided to settle all outstanding issues including Pakistan bilaterally.[15] Confirmation of LoC, as border would turn Azad Kashmir to a full-fledged province of Pakistan, "something Bhutto possibly initiated when he came to power.[16]" Few even believe that Bhutto had offered to make 'AJK' a province of Pakistan.[17]

(iii) The administrative changes Bhutto brought about in Northern Areas, which is now better known as Gilgit-Baltistan (G-B or GB), almost turned the latter into the de facto fifth province of Pakistan. New administrative changes further integrated Gilgit-Baltistan into Pakistan.

(iv) People of the region as well as the Pakistani authorities had perhaps realised that annexing Kashmir by force was now impossible owing to India's size of military strength.

The 'AJK' Interim Constitution Act of 1974 introduced a parliamentary system with a Prime Minister as the executive head and an indirectly elected President. As the executive head of 'AJK,' the Prime Minister wielded restricted power because the real power was vested in a new body called 'AJK' Council chaired by the Prime Minister of Pakistan. The 'AJK' Council is vested with both legislative and executive powers.[18] Headed by the Prime Minister of Pakistan, it consists of 11 members, six of whom are elected by the 'AJK' Assembly and five are nominated by the Pakistani Prime Minister. The 1974 constitution thus took away most of the powers accorded to the 'AJK' assembly by 1970 Act and vested these in the 'AJK' Council. These included the power to appoint High Court and Supreme Court judges. The major sources of income for the 'AJK' Government, like income tax, were given away to the 'AJK' Council. The 'AJK' Government's power to appoint the Chief Election Commissioner and the Auditor General was also taken away.

A critical analysis of the Interim Constitution Act, 1974 indicates that the Act has not only allowed the Kashmir Council to function as a parallel government but has also led to problems in governance. In an email dated May 4, 2018, in response to a query from one of the authors, Jalaluddin Mughal, a senior journalist from Pakistan commented that Kashmir Council enjoyed "ambiguous status since it was established, and it was not a representative body of 'AJK' people because majority of its members were not elected by 'AJK' people." He held that the Council drew its authority not from the Interim Constitution Act of 1974, but rather from the 1949 Karachi Agreement, "which gives all powers to Pakistan government." He also pointed out that "neither the Act of 1974 nor the Karachi agreement was drafted, signed and ratified by any elected representative of the 'AJK' people"and even "now the 'AJK' Assembly does not have the power to amend the 1974 Act without prior approval of the federal government." That is why, he concluded, "the elected leadership of 'AJK' has been demanding [review] of all the agreements with Pakistan and to amend [the 1974 constitution] to empower the local elected government rather than operate through the 'AJK' Council, [which is not entirely representative of the will of the people of 'AJK']." While the 'AJK' Government remains accountable both to the Council and the Assembly, the Council is not accountable to either the 'AJK' Government or Accountability Bureau. According to Tanveer Ahmad, a PoK-based social activist, "'AJK' is a legal anomaly and the current governance structure in 'AJK' is most certainly not a structure, which accommodates accountability and transparency of any kind."[19] Even those matters that come under the purview of the 'AJK' Government are in effect run by the bureaucrats, the government in Islamabad controls their appointment. Senior civil servants – Chief Secretary, Additional Chief Secretary, IG Police, Finance Secretary Health Secretary, Auditor General and Accountant General – are appointed by the Pakistan government. While commenting on the loopholes of the Interim Act, a Pildat report maintains:

> This generates grievance among AJ&K services group who feel their powers having been curtailed in operation of even routine affairs. Known as 'Lent Officers,' and not being under the AJ&K Government's control in matters of discipline or posting, the posted officers are a strong check on the

> exercise of powers by the President and Cabinet of AJ&K. This system of 'Lent Officers' is a permanent feature, and has never been changed. The Government of Pakistan, therefore, always retained an extremely strong influence in AJ&K affairs.[20]

The Interim Constitution Act 1974 left the 'AJK' Government with very little power. The Act not only denied the political rights of the people by empowering the Kashmir Council more than the 'AJK' Assembly, but also marginalised the 'AJK' Government's power over the areas under its control.

On June 1, 2018, the President of 'AJK' assented to the 13th amendment passed by the joint sitting of Joint Session of 'AJK' Legislative Assembly and 'AJK' Council. This amendment seeks to transfer executive and legislative powers from 'AJK' Council to 'AJK' government, and create four more constituencies on the basis of the increased population. (For details see Appendix IV).

The controlled 'democratic' system in 'AJK' was resented by local leaders, even by those who supported Kashmir's final accession to Pakistan. It has denied political rights to the people by making the Kashmir Council more powerful than the legislative assembly. Pakistan found it easy to deal with these pro-Pakistan Muslim Conference leaders and therefore, it felt itself under no pressure to allow the people the right to decision making. There has never been a serious effort to install a political system where people would have their say in policy making. On various occasions, leaders of the Muslim Conference have criticised Pakistan's carrot and stick policy to woo or punish them. However, Pakistan has succeeded in patronising these leaders who advocate merging of entire Kashmir with Pakistan. However, a vocal constituency wedded to the idea of independence of entire Kashmir has also made its presence felt all along even if it has not been allowed to participate in the elections in 'AJK.' Such policies have "stifled the development of indigenous institutions" as Pakistan is obsessed with the idea of control of 'AJK' people and disallowed the local leadership to evolve any responsive system on their own lest they would veer towards independence. Therefore, the people have always been asked to wait for the promised plebiscite to resolve things. With the mainstream political parties in Pakistan making successful entry into the political scenario in 'AJK,' there has been regular emphasis on strengthening Pakistan's hold on AJK. This has shut the door on political dissent in 'AJK' and "meant that [AJK] did not develop any positive political alternatives, democratic or otherwise, to those on offer in Indian J&K."[21]

During the past 62 years, the people of 'AJK' have been unable to rise out of poverty in large measure because they are utterly under the brutal oppression of

Pakistan. For its entire 62-year history, it has depended on Pakistan for its economic and political survival. It does not even issue its own postage stamps. The land which their elders knew as a mountain paradise has been turned into a living hell. Of the four million people who inhabit the region, ninc out of 10 live in extremely impoverished conditions in rural areas. Population growth is excessive, at 2.4 per cent per year, and the average house holds no fewer than seven people. Sadly, 'AJKs' future is as murky today as it was in 1947 as it still lives under Islamabad's shadow.

Politics in Gilgit Baltistan: Quest for the Elusive Fifth Province

Gilgit Baltistan was referred to as the Northern Areas until 2009, by the government of Pakistan. It was given its present name when the Pakistan People's Party (PPP) government in Islamabad promulgated the 'Gilgit-Baltistan Empowerment and Self-Governance Order (GBESGO)' in 2009.[22]

As per this order, there is a Gilgit Baltistan Legislative Assembly[23] which has 24 directly elected members and a 15 member Gilgit Baltistan Council headed by the Pakistan Prime Minister. The council exercises virtual power in important spheres of governance. There is also a provision for a Gilgit Baltistan supreme appellate court in addition to the high court. These structures work under the overall control of the Federal Ministry of Kashmir Affairs and Gilgit Baltistan (KAGB). In May 2018, just before demitting office, the outgoing Pakistan Muslim League-Nawaz (PML-N) government headed by Shahid Khaqan Abbasi repealed the order of 2009 and came out with a fresh "Government of Gilgit-Baltistan Order, 2018" which promised to offer more power to the elected legislature in matters concerning local governance, but in reality, the central government in Islamabad retained its absolute control over decision making in all spheres of governance.[24]

Access to Gilgit Baltistan has been restricted for the outside world. Beyond the Chinese involvement in the region since mid-1950s, the international community has shown little interest in the region. Gilgit Baltistan has multiple problems—political, strategic, economic, social and cultural—which has not attracted much attention of the world. Eminent PoJK historian and political commentator Dr Shabbir Chaudhary who lives in exile in the UK writes in his book titled *Legal Status of Jammu and Kashmir: Realisation of Bitter Facts* that "everything in Gilgit- Baltistan is controlled by Islamabad. Even the school curriculum is written by them, and our children are not taught history of Jammu Kashmir."[25] He further writes that:

> "Gilgit-Baltistan was part of the princely state of Jammu and Kashmir until November 1, 1947

> when Major Alexander William Brown, the former political agent of the Gilgit agency, launched a coup against Maharaja Hari Singh and arrested Governor Brigadier Ghansara Singh. It was major Brown who actually replaced the state flag with the Pakistani flag and announced its accession to Pakistan. He had no power to take that decision, yet as Indian troops were pushing the Pakistani invading army out of Kashmir in October 1947, Brown acted in desperation in order to deny India the passage to central Asia."[26]

Dr Chaudhary argues that Gilgit-Baltistan and her dry port of Sost at the Pak-China border right up to the sea port of Gwadar in Balochistan are key to China's economic expansionist design. However, the militant insurgency in Balochistan has brought the 'China-Pakistan Economic Corridor' (CPEC) to a standstill. He belives that a massive military operation allegedly supervised by the Chinese PLA is under way to crush Baloch rebels. It is in this backdrop that China has been exerting pressure on the Pakistan government to make sure that CPEC is made foolproof in Gilgit-Baltistan. The solution to the issue, as perceived by the locals, is being dictated by China; it is to make GB into its 5th province and take full control of the administrative matters and intensify its plunder of local natural resources.

According to Chaudhury, another aspect of Pakistan's

attempt to incorporate GB into Pakistan stems from China's need to gain access to clean water from the glaciers in the area. In a book titled *Kashmir the Untold Story* co-authored by Iqbal Chand Malhotra and Maroof Raza the authors reveal that China's major rivers Yangtze and Yellow river are polluted hence they cannot be used for the purpose of manufacturing semiconductors. They believe that semiconductors are used extensively in mobile phones, cars, fighter jets, satellites and even naval ships and hence whoever will dominate the manufacture of semiconductors in the world market will rule the digital world. According to the book *Kashmir the Untold Story,* "Chinese strategists were interested in Shaksgam valley, which is home to over 242 glaciers."[27] It is therefore important for China to control the waters flowing into GB. Moreover, the attempt of incorporation of GB into Pakistan as a fifth province is a clear violation of the same UN resolutions Pakistan does not tire of citing, which designated GB as a disputed territory.

The political status of Gilgit Baltistan is not well-defined unlike that of J&K—the Indian part of the former princely state—which has a definite constitutional status. Till 05 August 2019, J&K had a Constitution of its own and it was granted a special status in Article 370 of the Indian Constitution. The 'AJK,' has a constitution of its own since 1974, which has largely operated as an Interim Constitution and the provisions contained in this constitution limit the power of the so-called AJK in a manner that its administration and politics are largely dependent on and controlled by the central government of Pakistan. It is neither 'azad' or independent nor has it been given provincial status within Pakistan. The GB region does not find mention in the successive constitutions of Pakistan. Reeling under political ambivalence and instability, GB has been politically very restive in recent decades. Pakistan has been experimenting with ad hoc rules and structures in the region and has consistently failed to provide concrete political solutions for the region and its people. Additionally, Pakistan has made PoJK safe haven not only for terrorists operating in Kashmir but also for those linked with international terror outfits like Al Qaeda. At least 55 training camps are said to be located in the region and their cadres number close to 5,000. The proximity of these camps to Kashmir and the terrain of the region make infiltration much more convenient especially during summers.

Muzaffarabad and Kotli are known epicentres of such camps and dreaded militant organisations such as Lashkar-e-Taiba (LeT) and Hizbul Mujahideen have their operational headquarters there. Terrorist camps are noted to be widespread in Bhimber, Bakryal, Balakot, Chawari, Kotli, and Mangla. Lashkar has two camps in Muzaffarabad –Abdul-Bin-Masud and Danna. Hizbul has one in Muzaffarabad and the other in Mangla. Jaishe-Mohammed also has a strong foothold in the region even though it operates chiefly from Balakot (North West Frontier Province).

Lack of Constitutional Status and Political Ambiguities in PoJK

For a brief period after 1947, Gilgit Baltistan was governed by the 'AJK' administration. However, since the Kashmir issue was heating up at the international level, Pakistan thought it would be appropriate to separate it from 'AJK.' This was done as per the Karachi Agreement of 28 April 1949 between the president of 'AJK,' Sardar Mohammed Ibrahim Khan, a minister without portfolio from Pakistan, Mushtaq Ahmed Gurmani and Choudhry Ghulam Abbas, the representative of the Muslim Conference. Intriguingly, the future of Gilgit Baltistan was decided without any consultation with the local leadership, leave alone their representation in the talks for the agreement. Since no signatory was a native of Gilgit Baltistan, they had no locus standi, de jure or de facto, to determine the status of the region. The 'AJK,' however, has consistently been trying to reassert its control over Gilgit Baltistan.

The 'AJK' Interim Constitution 1974 refers to Gilgit Baltistan as a part of 'AJK.' In 1972, the 'AJK' Legislative Assembly passed a resolution for reclaiming Gilgit Baltistan which was willfully ignored by the government in Pakistan.[28] Subsequently in 1992, the 'AJK' High Court admitted a petition and in 1993 ordered the government in 'AJK' to take control of Gilgit Baltistan. The order was challenged by the government of Pakistan in the 'AJK' Supreme Court and on 14 September 1994 the court delivered a landmark judgement that declared that Gilgit Baltistan was part of J&K and not 'AJK.' Notably, the 'AJK' had cited the Interim Constitution to prove that Gilgit Balitstan was part of 'AJK' but the court refused to accept this argument. Thereafter, On 28 May 1999, the Supreme Court of Pakistan, in another judgement, noted that it is incumbent on Pakistan to guarantee fundamental rights to the people of Gilgit Baltistan.

The Gilgit Baltistan Empowerment and Self-Governance Order of August 2009 consisted of a set of political reforms. Basically, the package was designed to create the impression of liberal self-rule in Gilgit Baltistan. Even as the order was packaged as empowerment, it failed to give the region a well-defined political status or any form of representation in the federal structure of Pakistan. This order was just another one in the series of paradoxes that have characterised Pakistan's policy towards this part of PoJK.[29] Some of the salient features of the governance package are as follows:

(i) Gilgit Baltistan Council as the virtual authority: Gilgit Baltistan has no representation in the federal government of Pakistan. But, the legislative council which exercises virtual powers in Gilgit Baltistan is headed by the prime minister of Pakistan. This leaves little scope for the popularly elected representatives of the legislative assembly (33 members—of whom 24 are directly elected) to exercise any authority. Besides, as in the case of the Interim Constitution of the so called 'AJK,' all office bearers in Gilgit Baltistan have to sign an oath of allegiance to Pakistan.

(ii) No legal or constitutional binding: The empowerment and self-government order is not legally binding as it is in the form of a presidential order. This is because Gilgit Baltistan is not part of the Pakistani constitution and is not represented in the federal government. The order, hence, can be rescinded at any time depending on the government of Pakistan and its orientation. Hence, its future remains uncertain.

(iii) Observer status: The chief minister of Gilgit Baltistan has been invited to the federal cabinet as an "observer." The region has no representation in the National Finance Commission (NFC) even though there is a provision in the 1973 constitution under the Article 160 (1) for the representation of a non-constitutional unit. Such participation is, however, illusory as the representative has no right to vote in a body where decisions are made by the majority.

(iv) Levy of taxes: Under the new framework, whereby Gilgit Baltistan was to apparently function as an administrative unit, it was expected to generate revenue by the levying of taxes. Previously, no taxes were levied in Gilgit Baltistan due to its undefined political status. But the government of Pakistan decided to introduce taxes on corporates, including registered firms and the salaried class. In the backdrop of the lack of governance and development, the decision further exacerbated the woes of the people.

(v) Restrictions on debate and discussion: The Gilgit Baltistan legislative assembly and the council cannot debate issues related to defence, finance, internal security and foreign affairs or question the conduct of the judges of the Gilgit Baltistan Supreme Appellate Court and the Chief Court.30 The budget is passed by the assembly but prepared by bureaucrats in Pakistan. The chief secretary in the ministry of Kashmir affairs is a Pakistani bureaucrat and the governor, a political appointee. Essentially, the approach is to erect a political system with pretentious organisational subsets – all of them having signed the bond of allegiance to Pakistan.

(vi) Easy access for settlers to the region: This order

> entitles outsiders who possess asset/assets and a local identity card to become the citizens of Gilgit Baltistan.

The governance and self-rule order is broadly perceived by locals as "a strategic move to defuse pressure of rights organisation." They hold that the popularly elected legislature is weakened and "willfully emaciated" and in spite of all the trappings, Gilgit Baltistan does not have a constitutional status. This governance order is transitory and can be easily revoked in future. The Human Rights Commission Pakistan (HRCP) in its observer report rejected the order in clear terms. The report in its comprehensive note stated:

> The Gilgit-Baltistan (Empowerment and Self-Governance) Order, 2009 generally fell short of the people's expectations. The people of Gilgit-Baltistan had expected that the region would either be made the fifth province of Pakistan or get an autonomous status or an interim constitutional set-up on the pattern of Azad Jammu and Kashmir. The Order has brought little meaningful change at any level as, through various devices, the final authority on all important matters is the federal government. Most of the political parties criticised the Order as mere eyewash.[30]

In the 2009 elections for the Gilgit Baltistan Assembly, votes were cast along sectarian lines. The Sunnis who enjoy state patronage feared losing their advantage, allegedly rallied with militant groups and their affiliates turning places like Gilgit and Skardu into "militarised ghettos." Pakistan feared that allowing the "ethnic nationalism" to prosper would "possibly rupture her geographic seam."[31] This order was resisted by all including traders associations, and the Gilgit Baltistan, Chamber of Commerce (GBCCI). In March 2012, the prime minister of Pakistan while chairing a meeting of the Gilgit Baltistan Council in Islamabad, noted that a special committee had worked out proposals for taxation in Gilgit Baltistan. The proposal, Gilani noted, would soon be implemented to meet the development requirements of the region. He further added that even as key departments such as electricity, forest and mineral developments were within the jurisdiction of the Gilgit Baltistan Council, they were placed under the supervision of the Assembly under a temporary arrangement. Reacting to this development, the chairman of the GBCCI, Javed Hussain, stated in a press briefing:

> "Until and unless Gilgit Baltistan was given proper representation in the Senate and the National Assembly of Pakistan, Islamabad would not be allowed to impose taxes on the people of the region."[32]

Hussain also accused the Pakistan government of having failed to formulate a concrete and consequential policy to promote trade and commerce in the region. A formal decision to impose taxes in Gilgit Baltistan was taken by the government of Pakistan around October 2011.[33] However, widespread criticism forced the government to defer it for some time. The chief minister of Gilgit Baltistan requested the prime minister of Pakistan to postpone the decision till such time that the region is given representation in the NFC.

GB: Political Unrest and Role of Nationalist Groups[34]

The absence of political status and lack of guaranteed rights in Gilgit Baltistan have led to a political churning in the region. Amidst indefinite uncertainty, the political yearnings of the local people have been voiced by a number of political/nationalist groups, who demand freedom from Pakistan's control. These political groups have unanimously opposed Pakistan's high-handedness even as they hold differing view on the future shape and structure of Gilgit Baltistan. While some demand complete freedom from Pakistan, others demand an 'AJK' like structure for Gilgit Baltistan. While "there are several incipient sectarian-based movements for the creation, in the present Gilgit Agency, of either an independent or an autonomous region"[35] the last few decades have seen a rise in the number and strength of these groups even as they face arbitrary arrests, illegal detention and a majority being forced to flee their homeland.

To further aggravate the situation the Inter-Services Intelligence (ISI) maintains a strong presence in the region. The Northern Areas Command or the Force Commander Northern Areas (FCNA), a key Pakistani formation is headquartered at Gilgit.[36] Skardu in Baltistan near the LoC is known to be heavily guarded by this command. The extent of ISI presence can be gauged by the fact that the nationalist leaders are always under close watch. Several leaders have been put under house arrest and during this they are under strict surveillance from the ISI. There have been several cases of detention for minor offences and unaccounted deaths in custody. According to reports, the army and the ISI maintain a strong presence in Gilgit Baltistan to prevent nationalists from organizing any mass movements- either secretly or openly. In April 2010, most members of the local nationalists groups who protested against the Karachi Agreement (signed in 1949), were forced into exile for three months.[37] However, it is pertinent to metion here that Pakistan, right from the beginning, did not consider Gilgit Baltistan same that of Azad Kashmir. Ashok K. Behuria, who is a keen observer and a well-known expert on the politics of Pakistan, brings to fore this fact by writing:

The people of Azad Jammu and Kashmir ('AJK')

> enjoy many more rights than the people of GB....If one sees the statistics, especially the socio-economic data, it gives a sense of how the people of GB were governed and deprived of many rights.....according to the Pakistan Institue of Peace Studies (PIPS), 14 per cent of the men in the area were illiterate compered to the 3.5 per cent of women. However the Government of GB puts the date very differently. As per their data, about 37.85 percent of people were literate out of which 52.6 percent were male and 21.65 percent female....even the date about GB is misleading which highlights the ugly plight of the people of GB.[38]

The plight of the people of GB is heart wrenching. They face the wrath of the Pakistani armed forces on a regular basis. They cannot even protest. Their rights are curtailed everday.

Politics of J&K in Comparison

Jammu and Kashmir, in comparison, has a well-defined political status in the constitution of India. It enjoys democratic rights and has progressed since then in all the developmental parameters. In life expectancy, Jammu and Kashmir is ranked third out of 22 States in terms of life expectancy. The former State had an average life expectancy of 73.5 years between 2012 and 2016 (in comparison, Kerala had the highest life expectancy of

75.1, while Uttar Pradesh had the lowest [64.8] and the national average was 68.7). Moreover, J&K stood eighth in terms of poverty rate (10.35 per cent, while in c omparison, Goa had the lowest poverty rate of 5.09 per cent, and Chhattisgarh had the highest poverty rate of 39.93 per cent against the national average of 21.92 per cent. Similarly, in terms of Human Development Index (HDI), J&K is doing fairly well. In 2017, Jammu and Kashmir's HDI score was 0.68, higher than even States like Andhra Pradesh and Gujarat, while Kerala had the highest score (0.77) while Bihar had the lowest (0.57). The HDI is a composite index of life expectancy, education, and per capita income indicators. Furthermore, the National Sample Survey Office (NSSO) data shows average Kashmiri household spends more on recreational goods and rural Kashmir fares much better than rural areas of rest of India. The Observer Research Foundation analyzed the NSSO data to understand the spending patterns of the households of the Kashmir valley under various data points. The data was taken from the Household Consumer Expenditure Surveys conducted by the NSSO. The study chose the data from the years of intense conflict, beginning from the 1990s, to the most recent round of the survey to understand the economic well-being of Kashmiris. Despite the conflict,[39] the data shows that the consumer expenditure in the valley witnessed increase in tandem with, and in some cases surpassed the national average patterns. Over the last three decades, the overall household expenditure of an average Kashmiri household was over and above the average household in the country.

All these developmental parameters of Jammu and Kashmir are more than that of PoJK and it clearly shows that Jammu and Kashmir has progressed enormously under Indian union.

Religious freedom in PoJK and Jammu and Kashmir

Sectarianism in Gilgit-Baltistan has deep roots in history with religious, political and geo strategic connotations. Two developments played an important role in the emergence of sectarianism in Pakistan. One was the 1979 Iranian Revolution and the other was the Islamisation project of Zia-ul-Haq. In order to stem the Iranian influence in the region, Saudi Arabia funded the anti-Shia madrassas, outfits and regimes. Pakistan became the battle ground for the Sunni-Shia proxy war played by Iran and Saudi Arabia. The Shia revolution in Iran spurred the Shias in Pakistan, and Gilgit-Baltistan in particular. They demanded curriculum and textbooks similar to that of Iran; started going to Iran in large numbers for pilgrimage and also joined madrassas.

The sectarian feud started with religious leaders criticising and demonising the other sects in Friday sermons and other religious gatherings. Initially, the sectarian violence was limited only to the Gilgit district. The first clash erupted in 1983, over a dispute on the sighting of the moon. The Shia community ended fasting and started celebrating Eid on the declaration of moon sighting by their religious leaders. On the other hand, Sunnis did not end fasting. This was a major breach as Muslims are not allowed to fast on the day of Eid. Tensions quickly erupted and resulted in a bloody skirmish between the two groups. Sectarianism again erupted in May 1988 when the Shias in Gilgit protested against the Sunni-dominated administration for being lenient towards Sunni extremists. In retaliation, a religious militia from outside, in connivance with the state, massacred the Shias.

The offensive was apparently triggered by rumors of a Sunnis massacre in Gilgit by Shias, "deliberately spread to provide an excuse for Sunni militants to conduct the attacks."[40] An eyewitness in an interview to the International Crisis Group (ICG) revealed, "The laskhar consisted of thousands of people from Mansehra, Chilas, Kohistan and other areas in NWFP. They had travelled a long distance to reach Gilgit, but the government did not stop them. No government force intervened even as killings and rapes were going on. Instead, the government put the blame on RAW (Research and Analysis Wing, India's Intelligence Agency), Iran and CIA (Central Intelligence Agency.)"[41] This carnage against the Shias marked a watershed moment in the history of Gilgit-Baltistan. After this mayhem, Shias in Gilgit-Baltistan realised how vulnerable they were against well-organised and well-equipped Sunni militant groups. They started looking for help and Iran was a natural ally that could provide financial and material aid.[42] Furthermore, on August 17, 1993, 20 people were killed in riots in Gilgit on the occasion of Zia's death anniversary, as Shias, who are in a majority there, felt threatened by the large influx of Sunnis from other provinces, particularly from Punjab and Khyber Pakhtunkhwa. On 3 June 2004, another sectarian clash ensued on curriculum grounds.[43] Shias objected to the Islamiyat (Islamic Studies) syllabus, as they felt that the texts and images were presented in a strictly Sunni way.[44] When the controversy was not resolved, sectarian clashes erupted in Skardu.

Whenever the situation in the region gets out of hand, army is called in to control the situation. But clearly military intervention is not a long-term solution, and sectarian killings have not come to an end. From 1988 to 2010, 117 sectarian-related murder cases were recorded; 44 were recorded in 2011 alone.[45] In 2012, just to mention three incidents: 18 Shias were killed on 28 February on the KKH in Kohistan district while returning from Iran; 20 people were killed in Chilas on 3 April; and 100 people were killed in August while commuting between Islamabad and Gilgit.[46] However, since 2013, the region has seen some respite in sectarian and terrorist violence. Analysing the impact of sectarianism in Gilgit-Baltistan, Izhar Hunzai aptly states, "The development over the past three decades have left underlying sectarian tensions in Gilgit-Baltistan to simmer and grow. People increasingly think in sectarian terms and perceive the so-called other as problematic."[47]

On the other hand, the Valley of Kashmir is well-known for its plural tradition and syncretic culture. In fact, plurality has been an intrinsic feature of Kashmiri life for centuries. This includes ethnic, religious, and linguistic plurality. And this is the main reason that explains why the members of National Conference (NC) chose secular and Democratic Party of congress over Muslim league. Though Pakistan tried every way possible to create sectarianism in Kashmir for creating trouble but it failed to do so. Even the growing wave of separatist politics during the 1990s in Kashmir could not wipe out the Indian sentiment of adhering to democratic principles in Kashmir. Without challenging the relevance of separatist politics around the larger issue related to conflict and its resolution, the political actors in the democratic space had restricted their role mainly to the 'politics of governance' and as per Rekha Chowdhary, it is in the distinction between the two spheres of politics (the democratic sphere of 'politics of governance' and the separatist sphere of 'politics of conflict resolution') that one can find much explanation as to how the democratic space which had been delegitimised in the post-1989 period became so vibrant after 2002 that even the separatists had to acknowledged its reality.[48]

Endnotes

1 The people of Gilgit-Baltistan have been highly dissatisfied with the Pakistan government with the way people of 'AJK' enjoy rights. From the very beginning, Pakistan wanted only to swallow the region. They did this by sending a *Tehsildar* to take care of the region. Later the managed the region through the Ministry of Kashmir Affairs. During 1980s and 1990s, Pakistan controlled GB through some sort of rudimentary representative system. And the deprivation of GB people still lingers on. For more, see, Ashok k. Behuria, *Developments in Gilgit-Baltistan: Interpreting Local Angst*, in Ashish Shukla's edited book *Gilgit-Baltistan under Pakistan's Occupation,* Indian Council of World Affairs, New Delhi, 2021.

2 Surinder Kumar Sharma, Yaqoob ul Hassan and Ashok Behuria, *Pakistan Occupied Kashmir: Politics, Parties and Personalities*, Pentagon Press LLP, New Delhi, 2019, p. 1-2.

3 Ershad Mahmud, "Status of AJK in Political Milieu," *Policy Perspective*, 3 (2), 2006, accessed May 22, 2022 at http://www.ips.org.pk/education/1115-status-of-ajk-in-political-milieu.html.

4 Navnita Chadha Behera, *Demystifying Kashmir*, Pearson Longman, USA, 2007, p. 172.

5 Surinder Kumar Sharma, Yaqoob ul Hassan and Ashok Behuria, *Pakistan Occupied Kashmir: Politics, Parties and Personalities*, Pentagon Press LLP, New Delhi, 2019, p. 3.

6 Christopher Snedden, *The Untold Story of the People of Azad Kashmir*, p. 90.

7 Ershad Mahmud, "Status of AJK in Political Milieu."

8 Samuel Baid, "Azad Kashmir," Jasjit Singh (ed.), *Pakistan Occupied Kashmir: Under the Jackboot*, Cosmo Publications, New Delhi, 1995, p. 87.

9 See "Appendix II," *Karachi Agreement*.

10 Surinder Kumar Sharma, Yaqoob ul Hassan and Ashok Behuria, *Pakistan Occupied Kashmir: Politics, Parties and Personalities*, Pentagon Press LLP, New Delhi, 2019, p. 5.

11 Ibid.

12 Ibid., p.6.

13 Christopher Snedden, *The Untold Story of the People of Azad Kashmir*, p. 93.

14 Surinder Kumar Sharma, Yaqoob ul Hassan and Ashok Behuria, *Pakistan Occupied Kashmir: Politics, Parties and*

Personalities, Pentagon Press LLP, New Delhi, 2019, p. 8.

15 See, Simla Agreement at Appendix III.

16 Christopher Snedden, *The Untold Story of the People of Azad Kashmir*, p. 101.

17 Ershad Mahmud, "Status of AJK in Political Milieu."

18 The Azad Jammu & Kashmir Interim Constitution Act, 1974, amended up to date and Modified up to September 2005, Azad Govt. of the State of Jammu and Kashmir, accessed June 1, 2022, at URL: www.ajkassembly.gok.pk/ajkinterimconstituionact1974.pdf.

19 Javid Hayat, "Shadow Governance: Right to Vote and Rule in Azad Jammu & Kashmir- Analysis," *Eurasiareview*, July 23, 2012, accseesed June 23, 2022 at URL: http://www.eurasiareview.com/23072012-shadowgovernance- right-to-vote-and-rule-in-azad-jammu-kashmir-analysis.

20 PILDAT, "Pakistan-Azad Jammu & Kashmir Politico-Legal Conflict," *PILDAT*, September 2011, p. 16, accessed at URL: www.pildat.org.

21 Christopher Snedden, *The Untold Story of the People of Azad Kashmir*, p. 117.

22 Surinder Kumar Sharma, Yaqoob ul Hassan and Ashok Behuria, *Pakistan Occupied Kashmir: Politics, Parties and Personalities*, Pentagon Press LLP, New Delhi, 2019.

23 The Gilgit Baltistan Legislative Assembly (GBLA) consisted of 33 members of which Twenty-four members are to be elected directly on the basis of adult franchise; six women members are to be elected in accordance with the system of reserved seats in Pakistan. One additional seat (total 7)

was allotted to the newly created district of Hunza Nagar. And three technocrats and professional members are to be elected on the lines of reserved seats in Pakistan.

24 Ashok k. Behuria, *Developments in Gilgit-Baltistan: Interpreting Local Angst*, in Ashish Shukla's edited book *Gilgit-Baltistan under Pakistan's Occupation*, Indian Council of World Affairs, New Delhi, PP. 36-37.

25 Shabbir Chaudhary, Legal Status of Jammu and Kashmir: Realisation of Bitter Facts, Author House UK, 2020.

26 Ibid

27 Iqbal Chand Malhotra and Maroof Raza, *Kashmir's Untold Story*, Bloomsbury India,2019, p. 154.

28 Navneeta Chadha Behera, *Demystifying Kashmir*, Pearson Longman, 2007, p. 176.

29 Ashok k. Behuria, *Developments in Gilgit-Baltistan: Interpreting Local Angst*, in Ashish Shukla's edited book 'Gilgit-Baltistan under Pakistan's Occupation', Indian Council of World Affairs, New Delhi, 2021.

30 *Gilgit-Baltistan Elections 2009*, Report of HRCP Observers Mission, January 2010.

31 Senge H. Sering, *Constitutional Impasse in Gilgit- Baltistan (Jammu and Kashmir): The Fallout*, p. 357.

32 "GB traders to protest tax imposition," *Chitral Today*, accessed May 10, 2022 at URL: http://chitraltoday.net/gb-traders-to-protesttax-imposition/

33 Shabbir Mir, "Revenue generation: Govt formally decides to tax Gilgit-Baltistan," *The Express Tribune*, October 2,

2011, accessed June 10, 2022 at http://tribune.com.pk/story/264830/revenuegeneration-govt-formally-decides-to-tax-gilgit-baltistan/

34 The term Nationalist is used here to denote collectively or otherwise the pro-autonomy, pro-independence and the ethno-nationalist groups in Gilgit Baltistan.

35 The UN Refugee Agency (UNHCR), "Azad Kashmir and the Northern Area," Refworld, accessed May 30, 2022 at https://www.refworld.org/docid/3ae6a83ac.html.

36 "Pakistan Army Strategy in Gilgit Baltistan" accessed June 30, 2022 at URL: http://www.balawaristan.net/Latest-news/pakistan-army-strategy-in-gilgit-baltistan.html.

37 "11 nationalists banished from Gilgit Baltistan," *Weekly Baang*, Volume-03, Issue-10, 2010, accessed May 25, 2022 at http://weeklybaang.blogspot.in/2010_05_02_archive.html

38 Ashok k. Behuria, *Developments in Gilgit-Baltistan: Interpreting Local Angst,* in Ashish Shukla's edited book 'Gilgit-Baltistan under Pakistan's Occupation,' Indian Council of World Affairs, New Delhi, 2021, p. 33-34.

39 It is Pakistan alone which doesn't want conflict to end. This has been pakistan's (ISI's) strategy to motivate differen groups, arm them and instil in them the urge to fight against India for the sake of fellow Muslims. Even the Islamic parties want the Pakistani army to continue the Jihad in Kashmir. Currently pakistan is involved in targeted killing in Kashmir. This is a new plan of Pakistan

to spread unrest in Kashmir. It is believed that its purpose is to sabotage the resettlement plans of Kashmiri Pandits in Jammu and Kashmir after the abrogation of Article 370. Since the abrogation of Article 370, incidents of targeted killings have increased in Kashmir, especially in which terrorists have made soft targets of Kashmiri Pandits, migrant workers, and even local Muslims working in the government or police. Indian intelligence agencies believe that ISI is spreading propaganda among Kashmiri people that after the abrogation of Article 370, migrant workers coming from outside will take over their jobs and lands. Through this propaganda, they are again trying to garner support for pro-Pakistan terrorist organizations in Kashmir and disrupt peace in the valley.

40 Izhar Hunzai, "Conflict Dynamics in Gilgit-Baltistan," *United States Institute of Peace*, Special Report 321, January 2013, p. 5.

41 International Crisis Group, *The State of Sectarianism in Pakistan,* Asia Report, No. 95, April 18, 2005, p. 19., accessed April 30, 2022 at http://www.files.ethz.ch/isn/28410/095_the_state-of-sectarianisminpakistan

42 Ibid, p. 6.

43 Successive Pakistan governments under the garb of development have undertaken an exercise to change demographic composition of Gilgit Baltistan and local Shia population has been reduced to less than 50 per cent compared to 1948. Barrister Hamid Bashani, a native

from POK and a Human Rights Advocate said that G-B people have been agitating against the abolition of state subject law by Pakistan which has adversely affected the demographic character of G-B. These changes, he said, can be gauged by observing Shias who constituted more than 80% of G-B population in 1948 have now been reduced to less than 40%. The locals have agitated, protested and frequently raised demands seeking constitutional and political rights. These protests, he said have been met with brute force. Making a mockery of system, the aspiring candidates are "pre-screened" to ensure entry of only those who support annexation with Pakistan and can contest elections. Voices for Rights in Gilgit Baltistan are suppressed by law enforcement agencies and the nationalist leaders are subjected to torture and imprisonment for peaceful protests. For more, see, Dipanjan Roy Chaudhury, "Shia majority reduced to minority in Gilgit Baltistan: Barrister Hamid Bashani," 2020, accesed June 20, 2022, at URL: https://economictimes.indiatimes.com/news/politics-and-nation/shia-majority-reduced-to-minority-in-gilgit-baltistan-barrister-hamid-bashani/articleshow/79183272.cms?from=mdr

44 Georg Stober, *Religious Identities Provoked: The Gilgit 'Textbook Controversy' and its Conflictual Context*, International Schulbuchforschung, 29, 2007, p. 390.

45 "At Least 20 Shias pulled off Bus, Shot Dead in Northern Pakistan," *Dawn*, August 16, 2012, accessed

July 10, 2022 at www.dawn.com/2012/08/16/several-forced-off-buses-killed-in-northern-pakistan

46 "Pakistan Shias Killed in Gilgit Sectarian Attack," BBC, August 2012, accessed June 30, 2022, at URL: www.bbc.com/news/world-asia-19280339

47 Izhar Hunzai, *Conflict Dynamics in Gilgit-Baltistan*, United States Institute of Peace, Special Report 321, January 2013.

48 Rekha Chowdhary, *Jammu and Kashmir: 1990 and Beyond: Competitive Politics in the Shadow of Separatism*, Sage, 2019, p. 7.

CHAPTER IV

The State of Economy

The Economy of PoJK

THE ECONOMY of PoJK is majorly agrarian and is estimated to be around US$ 12 bn in size as of 2021. The annual budget for 2021-22 approved by the PoJK government was PKR 141 bn (US$730 million). Agriculture continues to be a major source of activity in the region, especially in PoJK, with low-lying plain areas involved in cultivating different crops like maize, millet, wheat, and barley, apart from various fruits and vegetables. Cattle grazing forms a significant means of subsistence in mountainous regions. Handicrafts, including carpets, rugs, shawls, and papier-mâché, also contribute to the economic subsistence of the region.

The Northern Areas of Gilgit-Baltistan have a trade economy, though agriculture and tourism contribute significantly to its economic health. Besides these traditional sectors, because of the region's exotic landscape and scenic beauty, tourism also contributes to the economic wellbeing of the region. A significant share of the PoJK economy is also sustained by the large sums of remittances from the Kashmiri diaspora community, mostly from the Mirpur division and predominantly settled in the United Kingdom. Hydropower generation could become a source of revenue for the AJK government, wherein surplus energy can be sold off to the other Pakistani provinces, which the Pakistani Government takes for itself.

Table 2.1 Summary of Socio-Economic Indicators in PoJK	
GDP at Current Prices (2020-21)	6.5 bn
Growth of GDP (2020-21)	0
Net Provincial Domestic Product (NPDP) at Current Prices (2020-21)	0
NPDP at Constant Prices (2020-21)	0
Growth of NSDP at Constant Prices (2020-21)	0
Per capita GSDP (2007-08)	US$ 1512
Fiscal Deficit	NA
Poverty (2016)	24.9 per cent
National Highway length (2020-21)	267 km
Rail Length 2020-21	0 Kms.

Per Capita Health Expenditure (2004-05)	NA
Key Industries	Beverages, Pharmaceutical and Auto, carpet weaving, Woodworking, handloom, agriculture,
Prospective Industries	Small & Cottage Industries, agriculture, Tourism, Handicrafts, Handloom, Mineral and Forest-based Industries, Hydel Projects
Main Industrial Cities	Mirpur, Muzaffarabad
Investment environment^	NA
Composite ranking of the state#	NA
Agriculture^	NA
Macro economy^	NA
Infrastructure^	NA

Source: For POJK the source of data for both 'AJK' and 'GB' are from respective government websites.[1]

The Economy of Jammu and Kashmir

Like PoJK, the economy of Jammu and Kashmir is predominantly agricultural, with a substantial contribution from the services sector. The Gross State Domestic Product (GSDP) of the state by 2020-21 stood at US$ 24.28 bn. The per capita GSDP of the state is estimated at around US$ 825. The major sectors of the economy are agriculture and allied, services and industries. The services sector contributed 62.63 per cent to J&K's Gross State Value Added (GSVA) in 2020-21, followed by the industry (19.3 per cent) and agriculture and allied industries (18.07 per cent) sectors, with the Services sector witnessing the fastest growth among the three sectors. The industry sector expanded at a CAGR (Compound Annual Growth Rate) of 5.84 per cent from 2011-12 to 2020-21, driven by manufacturing, construction, electricity, gas and water supply. In terms of budgetary allocations, Jammu Kashmir's 2022-23 annual budget was pegged at around US$ 15 billion.

Table 2.2 Summary of Socio-Economic Indicators, Jammu & Kashmir	
GSDP at Current Prices (2020-21)	22 bn
Per capita GSDP (2018-19)	US$ 825
Poverty (FY2008-09)	12.58 per cent
National Highway length (2020-21)	2423 Kms.
Rail Length 2021	356 Kms.
Per Capita Health Expenditure (2017-18)	US$ 40
Key Industries	Tourism, Handicrafts, Sericulture, Handloom, Horticulture, Food Processing & Agriculture.
Prospective Industries	Floriculture
Main Industrial Cities	Srinagar, Jammu & Kathua
Investment environment	4th rank

Composite ranking of the state	8th rank
Agriculture	15th rank
Macro economy	3rd rank
Labour laws (2009)	4th rank
Infrastructure	10th rank

Source: For J&K the source of the data is from J&K official government website.[2]

Over time, J&K has added new sectors to its economic basket, with tourism, floriculture, and horticulture making significant gains. These have become important domains of the local economy, inviting attention from the Government and market alike. This has resulted in the improvement of socio-economic indicators of the state and transformed the lives of people.

The diverse topography and climate ensure that different regions boast of diverse economic sectors within the state. In Kashmir valley, apart from rice cultivation, the other prominent sectors include sericulture, fisheries, horticulture and floriculture. Some of the well-known products from the region include Kashmiri Willow for cricket bat making, saffron, apples, almonds, trout fishes, corn, millet, barley, cherries, peaches, and pears. A vast natural resource base has allowed the state to divert the land usage for cultivating major fruits. Consequently, horticulture has emerged as a significant sector in the state's economic transformation. This sees an annual turnover of around US$ 1.2 bn across with over 3.5 mn people associated with the sector directly or indirectly.[3] Kashmiri handicrafts, including pashmina shawls, carpets, silks, rugs, copper and silverware, basketry, papier-mâché and pottery, are a significant source of export products from the region to the outside world.[4]

J&K's handicrafts are globally renowned, and hence the traditional handicraft industry has emerged as a large industry. Due to its large employment base and export potential, the industry has received priority attention from the government. The UT is also famous for its small-scale and cottage industries such as carpet weaving, silks, shawls, basketry, pottery, copper and silverware, papier-mâché, and walnut wood. The cottage handicrafts industry provides direct and gainful employment to around 340,000 artisans.

In the Jammu region, high-quality Basmati rice, maize, and corn are grown abundantly. Besides, the region forms the backbone of the manufacturing sector of the state economy, with several industrial belts established over time. Despite the major impediments in the form of topography, the Government has formed special economic zones and accordingly established industrial parks in almost every district of the state.

The state is bestowed with a beautiful natural landscape encompassing lakes, meadows, peaks, and religious sites for different communities. This attracts millions of tourists to the state round the year and has consequently become a significant contributor to the local economy benefiting hundreds and thousands of people directly and indirectly. This has pushed the Government to fast pace infrastructural establishment to further develop and promote Jammu and Kashmir as the primary tourist destination in India and internationally. In the domain of religious tourism, the state attracts millions of pilgrims to different shrines from different communities alike.

Table 2.3 Comparative Analysis of the Socio-Economic Indicators of J&K and PoJK

Indicator	J&K	PoJK
GSDP at Current Prices	US$ 22 bn	US$ 6.5 bn
Per capita GDP	US$ 825	US$ 1512
Poverty	12.58 per cent	24.9 per cent
HDI	0.68	0.61
National Highway length	2423 Kms.	262Kms of Strategic Highways
Rail Length	356 Kms.	0 km
Per Capita Health Expenditure	US$ 40	NA
Key Industries	Tourism, Handicrafts, Sericulture, Handloom, Horticulture, Food Processing & Agriculture.	Beverages, Pharmaceutical and Auto, carpet weaving, Woodworking, handloom, agriculture

Prospective Industries	Floriculture, fisheries, floriculture	Small & Cottage Industries, agriculture, Tourism, Handicrafts, Handloom, Mineral and Forest-based Industries, Hydel Projects
Main Industrial Cities	Srinagar, Jammu & Kathua	Mirpur, Muzaffarabad
Unemployment	24.6 per cent	10.3 per cent

Source: For J&K the source of the data is from J&K official government website. And for PoJK the sources of data for both 'AJK' and 'GB' are from respective government websites.[5]

The above basic economic indicators of J&K and PoJK evidence a gross mismatch. Take, for instance, the budgetary allocations by the governments of India and Pakistan for J&K and PoJK, respectively. For the financial year 2021-22, India allocated around US$ 15 bn for J&K against Pakistan's US$ 1.27 bn for the same period. This translates into India spending around 12 times the financial capital for the development of J&K against Pakistan's meagre spending in PoJK. From the table above, it is evident how J&K's GDP at US$ 22 bn stands around four times PoJK's US$ 6.5 bn, despite Pakistan's continued belligerence in J&K on account of a three-decade-long proxy war through sponsored militancy. In terms of poverty, J&K, with its 12.58 per cent poverty rate, does not only trample the PoJK's 24.9 per cent by half but is way above other Indian states on account of positive governmental initiatives, especially the landmark land reforms in the 1950s only. Conspicuously, neither has Pakistan done any land reforms in its mainland provinces but remains so in PoJK, which has meant that the country as a whole remains feudal and oppressive in character. Pakistan has not even developed a proper road network in PoJK, with just 267 Kms of what it calls Strategic Highways, which are primarily for military purposes rather than local development.

In comparison, India has expanded the National Highways network throughout J&K, which presently stands at around 2500 Kms. Pakistan has even denied PoJK rapid transportation systems like railways even after 70 years of occupation of the territory, which reflects its colonial mentality to deny the people basic infrastructure. The indicator where PoJK scores over J&K is the per capita GDP, which is US$ 1512 and US$ 825 for these regions, respectively. However, there is a catch in this, as it is mostly because of the external remittances from the large displaced Kashmiri population, who were forced out of the region from the 1970s onwards as Pakistan started exploiting the resources of the state through projects like Mangla Dam in Mirpur.

Sectors of Economy

PoJK region is home to vast reserves of natural resources, which predominantly include marble and granite besides copper, gold, silver and coal. It also has reserves of precious stones like rubies, sapphire and tourmaline. Despite this vast mineral base, the PoJK government has been unable to exploit these in the absence of any worthwhile infrastructure and lacks capital inflow to procure advanced tools and train the required human resources.

In contrast, Jammu and Kashmir hold significant reserves of minerals, including 6081 million tonnes of limestone, 150 million tonnes of gypsum, 400 million cubic meters of marble, 5.2 million tonnes of granite, 8.6 million tonnes of bauxite, 9.5 million tonnes of coal, 8 million tonnes of lignite, 7 million tonnes of magnesite, 9.6 million cubic meters of slates, sapphires, 2 million tonnes of quartzite, 400 tonnes of the annual crop of borax, 12.37 million tonnes of dolomite, 28 Million tonnes of China clay, and 62 million tonnes of graphite. This makes it an opportune place to establish industrial units to exploit these resources.

Industrial Base

Jammu and Kashmir is a land-scarce and labour-abundant state, with less than 30 per cent of its total area suitable for cultivation. The majority of the land comprises mountains and hillsides. Despite that, the state has predominantly an agrarian economy, which makes the development of the industrial sector highly essential. The state does not enjoy a wide variety of mineral resources but is well endowed with some proven natural resources like limestone, gypsum, coal, lignite, quartzite, clay, Borax etc. The state is also rich in forest wealth and some industrially important agriculture and horticulture products. Due to temperate climatic conditions, Kashmir is the only place in the Indian union highly suitable for rearing Univoltine and Bio-voltine silkworm races, which are famous for high-quality silk. For sustainable development in the industrial sector, there is an equal need for peace and stability, but, unfortunately, the state has remained politically most unstable right from the beginning because of Pakistan's belligerence, which has seen the state endure a prolonged proxy war over the years, creating hurdles for the establishment of a well-developed industrial setup. The impact of conflict on the industrial health, as also the socio-economic life of the state, could be gauged from the fact that the industrial output of the SSI, Khadi and Village Industries (KVVIs), and Public Sector Industries (PSUs) declined to 1.2 per cent, 1.02 per cent, 0.82 per cent and -4.35 per cent respectively.

Over time, the government has been able to diversify the industrial base of J&K from the previously concentrated cottage sector to producing traditional and modern products. However, industrial growth in the state is pronounced more towards the small-scale sector than other sectors. Sector-wise, Small Scale Industrial (SSI) sector has achieved phenomenal growth and diversification over time. To further this, the J&K

has a well-established State Industrial Development Corporations (SIDCO) and Small-Scale Industries Development Corporations (SICOP), through which 53 industrial parks estates have been set up across districts, allocating subsidised spaces with round-the-clock electricity and other facilities. This has ensured that J&K prides itself on having Food Processing and Agro-based industries like Sauces, Ketchup, Fruit Juices, Jams, Jellies, Vegetable Juices, Puree, Pickles, Fruit Waxing, apart from Packaging, Grading, Leather Processing and Leather goods, Tissue culture, Silk Reeling Yarn and Yarn spun from silk waste, the woven fabric of silk or silk waste, Wool & woven fabrics of wool, Woven fabrics of cotton, Medicinal herbs-processing, Computer hardware/Electronics (integrated circuit & micro assemblies), Sports goods and articles and equipment for general physical exercise, Auto Ancillaries, Handicrafts, Precision engineering, and exploration of minerals, etc. One of the niche industries in Kashmir is the cricket bat-making industry. There are close to 300 big and small manufacturing units of cricket bats in the state, with each unit manufacturing on an average 25000 bats per annum at a price ranging from anywhere between US$ 3 to US$ 50 per bat. The industry exports nearly thousands of finished and semi-finished cricket bats. The sector overall contributes 12.55% to the overall GDP of J&K.

On the other hand, PoJK has a very nascent industrial

base. The main industrial towns in the occupied territory are Mirpur and Muzaffarabad. The most prominent industrial sector of the region is the cottage industry, with a substantial number of people associated with it. This includes weaving and embroidery of Kashmiri Shawls, Chaddar (Veil) Making, Gabba-Sazi, Namda-Sazi, Carpet Weaving, Papier-Mâché, wood carving, Tila Work, etc. The PoJK Government has set up AJK Small Scale Industries Corporation in the 1990s to "serves as an instrumental tool for entrepreneurship, micro-economic development, employment generation and poverty alleviation." However, the industrial output of the sector has remained very low and has failed to make a turnaround. Furthermore, as the industrial profile of the region evidences, PoJK lacks any substantial diversified industries base and therefore remains reliant on the import of almost everything from Pakistan and hence continued dependence on Islamabad and the Pakistani army, which interestingly owns companies across sectors and produces everything in Pakistan from mineral water to garments to processed foods.

Agriculture

As highlighted above, the diverse topography and climate ensure that different regions boast off diverse economic sectors within the state. Within this, agriculture forms a backbone of the economy of Jammu and Kashmir, with close to 70 per cent of the population directly or indirectly engaged with it or its allied sectors for livelihood and employability. This has been ensured by the revolutionary land reforms carried out in the state in the 1950s that allocated land in the hands of the masses, transforming them from feudal era peasants to small landholdings owners, thereby ensuring the majority of the population could grow their own foods. The state's major crops and other agricultural produce include rice, maize, wheat, saffron, barley, pulses, and oilseeds. Saffron is the most prominent agricultural export from the state worldwide because of its quality and medicinal values.

The continued efforts of the government have resulted in making the agricultural sector a sustainable and remunerative activity for the local population, notwithstanding the state's geographic positioning, harsh weather conditions, hilly terrain, small and fragmented land holdings, fragile soil in hilly areas susceptible to soil erosion, limits to mechanised farming and transportation of products, extreme limits to irrigation of cultivated land, single cropping season in temperate/high altitude areas, growing population, and inadequate and unorganised marketing infrastructure.

The government, however, through its concerted efforts and liberal capital spending in the scientific endeavours through two major agriculture universities in the state, has been able to arrest the negative impact of these disadvantageous factors. It has further improved the delivery of services like credit, and quality inputs, like seeds, fertilisers, farm machinery etc., which has resulted in better agricultural produce. The Government of India has also extended its various schemes to the state like National Food Security Mission, National Mission on Agricultural Extension & Technology, National Mission on Oil seeds & oil Palm, National Mission for Sustainable Agriculture, Catalytic Development Programme (Sericulture), Command Area Development & Water Management Programmes, Weather based crop insurance scheme, National Bamboo Mission, and importantly Rashtriya Krishi Vikas Yojana (RKVY). Under RKVY, the state receives incentives for its farmers to achieve and sustain inclusive growth, especially the flagship Saffron Mission.

The state has utilised the liberal funding from the Central Government through these schemes to improve the existing crops and produce and also widen their scope. This includes the focus on Organic Basmati Rice, Rajmash, off-season vegetables, potatoes, aromatic & medicinal plants, virus-free potato seeds for all seasons, development of commercial floriculture, production of virus-free quality seeds for flowers and vegetables, aromatic & medicinal plants, mushrooms round the year, honey and honey by-products, fodder intensification, boost to Quality Saffron Production, and Jatropha

(Biofuel) cultivation on wastelands and rainfed areas of Jammu region.

As an allied sector to Agriculture, J&K has witnessed a major shift to the horticulture domain, where the state has undergone revolutionary changes with an ever-increasing production of major fruits like apples. The sector contributes immensely to strengthening the financial condition of the State, poverty alleviation, and employment generation and is a core sector of Jammu and Kashmir agriculture. The variety of horticultural products of the State has earned worldwide fame because of its good quality and taste. The fruit crops grown in the state are apple, almonds, walnuts, pears, cherries and apricots in temperate areas and mango, citrus, litchi, papaya, guava, etc., in subtropical areas. Saffron cultivation in the state is unique in the world. As of 2021, the sector generates an annual turnover close to US$ 1.25 bn (INR 10,000 crore), with over 35 lakh people directly or indirectly dependent on horticulture.[6]

Compared to J&K, notwithstanding the agrarian nature of its economy and importance in the rural socioeconomic sector, the agriculture in the PoJK region operates at a subsistence level and is more of "Mountain Agriculture." According to a UNDP report, the total number of farms in PoJK is 277599, of which nearly 98% are small farms, meaning that the smallholders cultivate 90 per cent of the total cultivated area. According to a report by the PoJK Government's Directorate General of Agriculture, despite "good environmental conditions, soil and water resources," agricultural production in the region has stagnated.[7] Furthermore, a mere seven (07) per cent of the cultivable land is irrigated, with soil inherently weak, primarily deficient in nutrients essential to growing crops. The region is yet to experience modern technological interventions, with bullocks and ploughs continuing as the primary land tillers. The major crops cultivated in the region include wheat, maize, and rice. Major vegetables include tomatoes, beans, potatoes, spinach, turnip, karam, brinjal, radish, and others. Furthermore, the prominent fruits cultivated in the region include walnut, mango, apple, apricot, cherry and local pomegranate. However, given the subsistence level production, the sector is more or less producing a local level consumption quantity and is no surplus for the export and hence no revenue generation.

Banking sector

The financial market of the State is bank dominated. Banks are meeting the financial requirements, particularly of the unorganised sector and the self-employed in the micro and small business sectors (MSMEs). Infrastructure development, considered the key to the long-term sustainable growth of the economy, has heavy dependence on bank financing. The insurance sector, though well capitalised, is significantly exposed to the banking system. This accords banks a critical role in the present economic environment. More importantly, to achieve the objectives of a faster, sustainable and inclusive development agenda of the central government by providing access to banking to all the citizens, banks are broadening and deepening their network besides diversifying the domain of activities and jurisdiction. The banking structure of J&K comprises of public sector Banks, Private sector Commercial Banks, Regional Rural Banks and Central/State Co-operative Banks.

As of 2018, J&K had 2036 bank branches of the scheduled commercial banks, co-operative banks and state financial corporations (SFC) in operation in J&K. The share of scheduled commercial banks is 85.90 per cent, with 23.82 per cent of public sector banks, 45.68% of private sector banks and 16.40 per cent of regional rural banks. Furthermore, 13.41 per cent share is held by central/ state cooperative banks, and only 0.69 per cent is the share of state financial corporation (SFC). Their performance has been progressively improving regarding mobilisation of savings, deployment of credit, disbursement of microcredit under NABARD's Self-Help Group-Bank Linkage Programme supporting Government Programmes etc. In terms of banking presence, 52.5 per cent of the branches are in rural areas, 21.16 per cent in semi-urban and the rest 26.32 per cent are located in urban areas, respectively. On average, one bank branch is available per 6 thousand people. The banking density in J&K is 49.79 sq. km per branch for every 7000 people, which is below India's national average. The most prominent banks operating in the state include Jammu & Kashmir Bank (JKB), State Bank of India (SBI), Punjab National Bank (PNB), *Elaqa'i Dehati Bank* (EDB), Jammu and Kashmir Grameen Bank (JKGB), and HDFC Bank, among others.

JKB is the state's most prominent financial institution and is considered the backbone of its financial sector. It functions as the state's universal bank and as a specialised bank in the rest of India. The bank caters to the banking requirements of a wide population, including Business enterprises, government employees, semi-government and autonomous bodies, farmers, artisans, public sector organisations and corporate clients. It has a network of 957 business units and 1386 ATMs as of 2021, spread over 18 states and 4 UTs across the country, of which 833 are operating in J&K.

On the other hand, the financial sector of PoJK presents very modest statistics. The most prominent bank of PoJK is the Bank of AJK (BoAJK), which has 77 branches across the occupied territory. It is a wholly owned corporate entity of the PoJK Government, aimed at mobilising the private savings and public funds for diverting them to productive channels, promoting industrial, agriculture, rural micro-financing and other socio-economic activities. Apart from these, there are further 102 branches of Banks like HBL, Allie Bank, Mezaan Bank, MCB, Askari, and National Bank of Pakistan. Interestingly, aside from the fact that Pakistan propagates the PoJK region as the soca called Azad Jammu Kashmir (AJK) through the façade of non-existent regional autonomy, the financial services of the region remain under the direct control of the State Bank of Pakistan, which is the banker for the PoJK Government.

Tourism

Across both sides of the Line of Control, Jammu and Kashmir is enriched with fertile plains, towering mountains, breathtaking lakes, and gushing rivers.[8] As such, the state is bestowed with tremendous tourism potential. This sector, therefore, has the potential to contribute significantly to the local economy by generating both direct and indirect means of livelihood. In PoJK, every division is bequeathed with tourist destinations. In the Muzaffarabad division, the major attractions include Red Fort, Pir Chinassi, Patika, Subri Lake and Awan Patti. In the Neelum Valley division, these include Athmuqam, Kutton, Keran, Changan, Sharda, Kel, Arang, and Taobat. In Poonch, the major destinations are Banjosa Lake, Devi Gali, Tatta Pani, and Toli Pir. Likewise, in the Bagh district, these include Bagh Fort, Dhirkot, Sudhan

Gali, Ganga Lake, Ganga Choti, Kotla Waterfall, Neela Butt, Danna, Panjal Mastan National Park, and Las Danna. Besides, there is Mangla Lake (Dam) and Ramkot Fort in Mirpur. Furthermore, the prime locations include Leepa Valley and Sudhanoti. Despite the abundance of these tourist attractions, the region lacks a basic tourism infrastructure that deters tourists outside of PoJK from visiting these places.[9] There are no estimates from either the government or any organisation that could reflect people's association with this sector. In 2019, before the coronavirus pandemic struck, the region witnessed 1.5 million footfall of domestic tourists.

Gilgit-Baltistan also boasts of some of the best tourist destinations because of "its composite attractions reflected in culture, heritage, nature, adventure, sports, water, clean air, landscape, leisure, wildlife, and biodiversity."[10] The region's treasure trove includes some of the world's famous mountain ranges like The Himalayas, Karakorum and Hindukush. These mighty mountain ranges have five over 8000-meter peaks, including K2 (Mount Godwin-Austin), Nanga Parbat (Diamir), and another 101 over-7000 meters high peaks. The region hosts around 5100 Glaciers and 119 Lakes and has approximately 2200 sq. miles of snow-covered area.[11] Gilgit Baltistan has 23 historical Forts and around 65 Archeological sites of tourism interest. Though the GB government claimed an inflow of 700000 tourists in 2021,[12] the region lacks primary infrastructure, including the roads and hotels to support the tourism sector. The main arterial road to the region, the Karakoram Highway (KKH), remains poorly maintained, often blocked by landslides and lacks any other transport medium. Likewise, air travel infrastructure is abysmal, with infrequent sorties to the region's two small air stripes. The Pakistani Government has also securitised the inflow of international tourists, which mandates necessary security briefings before and debriefings after travelling to the region. This deters high spending foreign tourists from visiting the region.[13]

J&K, as already highlighted above, is famous for its splendid natural beauty and natural scenery throughout the world. The grandeur of the state, in particular, Kashmir valley, is enhanced by its gigantic snow-clad mountains, breathtaking valleys, beautiful lakes and springs, gushing rivers, lush green forests, pastures, meadows and beautiful health resorts, and picturesque landscapes. This has earned it the epithets like the "Paradise on Earth", "Switzerland of Asia", and "Crown of India", and invites millions of tourists annually. During the summer, one can enjoy the beauty of nature, trout fishing, big and small game hunting etc. during winter, climbing mountain peaks and sports like skating and skiing on snow slopes are commonly enjoyed. The tourism industry has been one of the worst affected sectors of the state's economy because of the ongoing

Pakistan-instigated armed insurgency in the last three decades. It hindered the smooth growth of this important sector as the security situation discouraged most travelers from visiting this most popular Himalayan destination, thereby the livelihood of thousands of people associated with it directly or indirectly. The political instability greatly altered the direction, flow, pattern and volume of tourists to J&K.

The state also has prominent shrines for different religious communities, which ensures the footfall of pilgrims from across India throughout the year. The J&K Government has promoted the state as a heritage tourism destination by interlinking different tourism domains like religion, culture, wildlife, adventure and eco-tourism to showcase the state's pluralist legacy across the globe. Some of the major tourist attractions in the state include world-famous resorts like Gulmarg, Pahalgam, Sonmarg, Patnitop, and Yusmarg and lakes like Dal, Manasbal, Wullar, Anchar, Nigeen, and Mansar, among others. There are dozens of Mughal-era gardens, including Shalimar, Harwan, Nishat, Parimahal, Chashma Shahi, Kokernag, Verinag, etc. In terms of sites and shrines of importance, Jammu and Kashmir boast of Amarnath Cave Shrine, Dargah Hazratbal, Mata Vaishno Devi Temple, Shahdara Sharif, Kheerbhawani temple, Chrari Sharif Makhdoom Sahib, Shankaracharya Temple, among others. There are many historical forts, prominently Hari Parbat Fort,

Amar Mahal Palace, Hari Niwas Palace, Mubarak Mandi Palace, Bahu Fort, and Ramnagar Fort, to name a few. Jammu and Kashmir Government, in recent years, established a chain of development authorities across the state to better the infrastructure of the existing tourist destinations while also tapping the new ones. This has brought new places to the state's tourism map, including Kaparan, Matigawaran, Duksum, Sinthen top, Margan top, Dusu, Aharbal waterfall, Peer Ki Gali, Lolab, Bungus, Doodhpathri, Mansbal among several others.

Before the Covid19 pandemic struck in 2020, Jammu and Kashmir witnessed a visitor footprint of around 16 million in 2019, according to available public data.[14] This includes foreign arrivals, domestic tourists and, importantly, religious tourists, a niche domain which has picked up over the years. In pilgrimage tourism, Vaishno Devi and Amarnath Cave shrine are the two most prominent destinations for the outside state tourists, with Vaishno Devi shrine alone attracting a phenomenal rush of devotees to the tone of 8 million in 2017-18 alone, while Amaranth cave attracted 2.60 lakh pilgrims in the same period. This signifies the importance of religious tourism in the state and contributes to different interlinking economic sectors. By June 2022 itself, the state has witnessed the arrival of around 8 million tourists, as revealed by the local Government.[15] In terms of budgetary allocations for 2022, the government earmarked US$ 98 million (INR 786 crores) for the further development of the tourism sector, including bringing 75 new tourist destinations on the tourism map of J&K.

The above analysis of the two regions manifests that while J&K has transformed the tourism sector into a full-fledged industry despite the continued Pakistani attempts to disturb the peace and security situation of the state, PoJK remains a modest beginning in every sphere, including importantly the infrastructure. It has failed to establish dedicated agencies and authorities like J&K to create basic tourism infrastructure in the region.

Fisheries

The state of Jammu and Kashmir is bestowed with large sources of water, which present it with the vast potential to expand the fisheries sector as a significant contributor to the local economy by generating employment. Modernisation, with active governmental interventions, and the growing economic status of the population coupled with changes in the social structures have had a major impact on the fisheries structure in the state. These positive interventions have resulted in over a three-fold increase in fish production in J&K. Government's liberal funding and subsidised loans have resulted in the development of a private fish-culture in the state, which has a significant commercial orientation and augmented the incomes of the people, particularly in the rural areas.[16]

Some of the major central government initiatives extended to J&K to incentivise the fisheries sector and make it a sustainable source of income and economic activity include (a) PM's package for the creation of employment opportunities, (b) Fisheries training and extension, (c) National welfare scheme for fishermen, (d) Rashtriya Krishi Vikas Yojana (RKVY) for blue revolution, and (e) Development of Inland Fisheries and Aquaculture. Along with these schemes, the government has spent significant capital to put the infrastructure in place through (a) Setting up of aquarium cum awareness centre, (b) Introduction of cage culture, (c) Setting up of fish farms, (d) Hatcheries for breeding, (e) Mahseer Fisheries, (f) Reservoir Fisheries, (g) Angling infrastructure. Some prominent farms established by the state government include National Fish Seed Farm Manasbal in the Ganderbal district and Trout Fish Farming Project Kokernag in the Anantnag district, among many others. One of the most significant interventions from the government to augment the private domain of the fisheries sector is the establishment of the Trout Feed Mill at the National Fish Seed Farm Manasbal in the Ganderbal district. Trout is a famous freshwater fish with a significantly high local and national demand. The region can potentially increase its stake in this sector because of large freshwater sources.[17]

Fisheries, one of the primary sectors of the state, contribute to the state's net domestic product, nutritional security and employment generation. It constitutes a major livelihood source for the economically backward population of the state. In absolute terms, the domestic product generated in the fisheries sector has increased appreciably from Rs 4.7 crore in 1980-81 to Rs 361 crore in 2015-16 at current prices, while the net domestic product (FSHNDP) to agricultural net domestic product (ANDP) has almost doubled.[18] Despite this, there is a need to expand the capital inflow in this sector to attract more locals, which can generate employment and livelihood avenues.

In the case of PoJK, the Jhelum, Neelum, and Poonch river systems present the potential to develop the fisheries sector. The common and famous fish varieties available in these water bodies include Snow Trout, Gulfam, Brown Trout, Rainbow Trout, Mahasheer, Rohu, Malli, Singhara, Grass carp, Silver Carp, Common carp, Big head, Mohri, Thalla, and Tilapia. The government in this occupied territory of J&K had launched the programme to "establish extension unit at each district level" in the public sector and help "establish 50 fish farms each year in the private sector" through funding and technical support, including supplying them with fish seeds. The government also intended to initiate fish farming in mini dams and promote integrated fish farming in the region. The PoJK, with the support of the United Nations (UNs) Foof and Agricultural Organisation (FAO), had announced to establish Fish Seed Production and Distribution Center in Mirpur, which has, however, not materialised yet.[19] A holistic study of the sector in the region exposes how the Governments of Pakistan and PoJK have failed to lay down the necessary infrastructure for the promotion of fisheries in the region and turn it into a sustainable livelihood sector for the population, grappling with limited employment avenues.

Handicraft

The handicraft sector occupies an important position in the economic structure of the state and has worldwide acclaim for high-quality craftsmanship, attractive designs and functional utility. A large section of the population, importantly women, are associated with and dependent on this sector for their livelihood sustenance directly and indirectly. Crafts like embroidery, shawls, crewel, namda, chainstich, woodcarving, papier-machie, Kani shawls, costume, jewellery and carpets hold a significant share in the overall production and export of the state. Silken carpets, in particular, constitute a speciality having no parallel in quality and design at the national level and, therefore, occupy an important position in the international market. The carpet industry is making a great contribution towards the foreign exchange earnings of the country. Notwithstanding the fact that Kashmiri arts and crafts have enjoyed worldwide fame and name, their production suffered to a large extent with the broke down of turmoil in the valley in 1989 at the best of Pakistan, which has derailed every sector of the state economy.

However, the continued affirmative actions of the government have rebounded the sector. During the year 2017-18 value of production of handicraft goods was estimated at Rs. 1930.75 crores, and handicraft goods valuing Rs. 1090.12 crores were exported. Apart from generating employment opportunities, the handicrafts sector makes the best possible use of locally available raw materials. Handloom is also the oldest and most widespread industry and has been a way of life in the state since time immemorial. It is the largest unorganised activity. The handloom sector in J&K is centuries old with specialised skills in manufacturing fabrics like pashmina shawls, ruffle shawls, shahtoosh shawls, silk sarees and other cotton items which have great demand in the national and international markets. The handloom industry of the state has a definite place of pride in the country.

On the other hand, the PoJK government has attempted to push handicrafts as an export from the region by establishing Handicrafts Development Centers in Muzaffarabad, Mirpur, Sharda, Neelum, and Haveli. Despite these interventions, it has failed to turn around this sector to promote it as an alternative and sustainable livelihood avenue. This is unlike J&K, where Pakistan has mastered in creating unrest by pushing through its Islamist proxies of varied orientations on an everyday basis.

Investment Opportunities in PoJK and J&K

Jammu and Kashmir, on account of its topography, meteorology, and hydrology, provide huge investment opportunities in various sectors. Despite this, PoJK has been unable to exploit its resources to attract investment. PoJK adopted Pakistan's Federal Industrial Policy, allowing all types of industries, except Arms & Ammunition, Security printing, Explosive material and radioactive material, in the region. It also adopted the policy of exempting industrial products from paying sales tax for five years, allowing protection to outside investors under the Economic Reforms Act 1992, and free transaction of principal amount and profits without prior permission of the Government for foreign investors, among other measures. Despite these inducements, PoJK has established just six Industrial Estates, with 1465 Industrial Units, medium & large-scale industries, in operation. Additionally, to appropriate the real Kashmir handicrafts, the PoJK government established Azad Kashmir Small Industries Corporation (AKSIC) in 1992, which has been unable to take off. At the same time, Gilgit-Baltistan lacks any formidable economic base, and as such, there are hardly any worthwhile industrial investments.

On the other hand, J&K has seen a steady inflow of capital from outside and a push by the Central Government of India to boost the investment climate. The state had to endure a vicious cycle of Pakistan-sponsored armed insurgency through its Islamist extremism ecosystem, which severely affected the socio-economic health of the state. Notwithstanding the extensive damage to J&K's infrastructure and loss of human resources, Pakistan's proxy war discouraged private investment and pushed the state's economy towards stagnation. Despite these setbacks in the last three decades, J&K has diversified its agriculture-based economy and expanded the capital inflow in the industrial landscape and tourism sector. Furthermore, the natural resource base supplemented with varied agro-climatic conditions has enabled the state to expand to horticulture and floriculture on a large scale, along with various agro-based industrial ventures. In terms of cultural artefacts, the state has devoted considerable capital to expanding the traditional handicrafts industry and taking the world-famous Kashmiri handicrafts to the global scale. The state invests substantial money in small-scale and cottage industries, including carpet weaving, silks, shawls, basketry, pottery, copper and silverware, papier-mâché, and walnut wood. For example, the export value of commodities; Jammu and Kashmir exported goods worth 188.18 million US dollars in 2019-20.[20] The Government has adopted a liberal industrial policy to attract industrial investments to the state. As part of facilitating the inward industrial investments, the state adopted a Single Window Clearance System to smoothen the process.

Furthermore, it offers liberal incentives and concessions to attract investments, including tax rebates and tax holidays. A special focus is being given to Information technology and related sectors and, as such, deems IT Software and IT services as part of manufacturing activity to provide it with industrial incentives. In April 2021, the J&K Government announced it had signed a record 456 memoranda of understanding (MOUs) with various firms for a potential investment worth US$ 3.17 billion.[21]

It goes on to establish how despite Pakistan's sponsored militancy which pushed major industrial investments out of the state, J&K has been able to turn around and attract more and more financial capital over the years. Pakistan has essentially transformed the region into a no-go zone for any outside investments that could help its inhabitants transform socioeconomically. Instead, Islamabad has undertaken a decades-long attempt to alter the region's demography by pushing the Punjabis to settle down in the region to put it under its lid. J&K's steady progress in attracting investment, including from major international financial agencies like Asian Development Bank (ADB), has been in the face of Pakistan's sponsorship of proxy war through the menace of militancy for the last three decades, which rendered the security situation untenable for the inflow for any major investments.

Physical Infrastructure

Towards having a comprehensive understanding of extreme disparities existing between Pakistan-occupied Jammu Kashmir (PoJK) on one side and Jammu and Kashmir (J&K) on the other, an exhaustive examination of different socio-economic and infrastructural indicators has been undertaken, including and not limited to roads infrastructure, civil aviation facilities, power generation and supply units, water supply, telecom networks, health, education and budgetary allocations. Furthermore, investment commitments made by Pakistan towards PoJK and the Central Government towards J&K are evaluated.

Modes of Transportation Roads

Road infrastructure is a primary factor determining the ease of penetration of goods and services to the nooks and corners of a country, region, or state. In essence, sustainable and inclusive economic growth calls for an efficient and extensive road network. Road infrastructure is critical for the sustainable growth of the economy besides industrialisation. In Pakistan Occupied Jammu Kashmir, the metaled road network, as of 2020, as per the Communications and Works Department of the PoJK

Government, stands at 8865 Kms. In addition, it also has another 8000 Kms of fair-weather roads in the region, totaling a road length of around 19000 Kms. This also includes 95 Kms of Strategic Highway, which is mostly used for the purpose of Pakistan's Army's movement. As per the Works Department of the provincial government, the Northern Areas of Gilgit-Baltistan have a metaled road length of 1394 Kms, Shingle Road length of 3726 Kms and Karakoram Highway of 460 KM, totaling 5580 KM across PoJK.

In comparison to the Pakistani-occupied territories, Jammu and Kashmir boast of an extensive road network across the length and breadth of the state. As per the Government of Jammu and Kashmir's Public Works Department (PWD), which manages the public infrastructure, the state's road network has increased to 42882 Kms by 2018, including 2584 Kms of National Highway.[22] It has seen an average of 107 per cent of the awarded cost of road projects by the Central Government, which signifies the Govt of India's importance to J&K towards its accelerated growth and transforming it into the model state in the country.[23] Road density for J&K state for the year 2016-17 is 34.81 kms per 100 sq. kms of the area and 245 kms per lakhs of population, the relative road density for the country for the year 2015-16 is 170 kms (on area) and 463 kms per lakh of population.

The arterial National Highway-44 connects the

capital cities of Srinagar and Jammu with the rest of the country. The Central Government has executed eight new fully funded National Highway projects to improve the connectivity in the state. The new Highways links Katra and Reasi, the base camps of Mata Vaishno Devi Ji and Shiv Khori shrine, Baltal and Pahalgam, the base camps of Shri Amarnath Ji shrine, Akhnoor and Sudh Mahadev in Jammu, border towns of Zanskar and Leh in Ladakh region and backward towns of Kupwara and Tanghdar. Three new Highways approved in Jammu included Domail-Katra-Reasi-Pouni, which has been named as NH No. 144, Jammu-Akhnoor-Nowshera-Rajouri-Poonch, named as NH No. 144-A and Batote-Chenani-Sudh Mahadev-Khelani-Doda-Kishtwar-Synthan-Khanabal, called as NH No. 244. Two new Highways approved in the Ladakh region are Kargil-Zanskar in Kargil district, which has been named as NH No. 301 and Leh-Debring-Mulden in Leh district, which has been named as NH No.3. Three new Highways approved for the Kashmir valley are Baramulla-Rafiabad-Kupwara-Tanghdar, named as NH No. 701, Baltal-Panchtarni-Chandanwari-Pahalgam-Batakut-Martand-Khanabal, named as NH No. 501 and Srinagar-Shopian-Qazigund, called as NH No. 444. Furthermore, the construction work on the strategic Z-Morh tunnel (6.5 kms) and Zojila tunnel (14 Kms) is underway to provide an all-weather road connection between Kashmir valley and

Ladakh, a long-standing demand of the people, which will provide further the economic and socio-cultural integration of these regions.

Further, keeping in view the developmental scenario of the state, the Central Government has proposed a 600-kilometre-long, Delhi-Amritsar-Katra controlled-access expressway to connect Delhi with Katra in Jammu & Kashmir via Amritsar, Moga, Sangrur in Punjab.

Railways

J&K state has rapidly expanded railway infrastructure in recent decades. The Jammu-Baramulla Railway link connects the Kashmir Valley with the Jammu Railway Station and the rest of the country. Currently, rail transport is available from Lakhanpur to Katra and Banihal to Baramulla. The construction of a 237 Km long rail line from Katra to Baramulla in Kashmir is near completion.

The Indian Railways has declared its Kashmir expansion project as a special project of National importance, with the central government bearing its costs on its own. On this track, the world's tallest railway bridge, Chenab Bridge, at the height of 359 m (1,178 ft), is nearing completion, which is the last leg to join Kashmir's railway line to the rest of the country. It will be an all-weather convenient and cost-effective mass transportation system in the state, which is expected to act as a catalyst for the state's overall socio-economic development, especially in the industrialisation of the region, as the movement of raw materials and finished products from J&K will speed up.

On the other hand, Pakistan has not extended any railway network to PoJK even after 70 years of controlling the territory, thereby denying its inhabitants the right to rapid transportation. This has contributed to withholding the region from undergoing any tangible development. This also highlights how Pakistan seems to keep PoJK underdeveloped to ensure its dependence on Islamabad.

Civil Aviation

PoJK has four small operational airports run by the Civil Aviation Authority of Pakistan. These include an airport at Muzaffarabad Airport, Rawalakot Airport, Gilgit Airport and Skardu International Airport. The airports at Muzaffarabad and Rawalakot, with their nascent infrastructure as mere air landing strips, have remained non-functional since the 2005 earthquake. This is despite a large number of PoJK residents, roughly 1.5 million as per governmental estimates, working and living abroad. This makes it explicit how the Pakistani Government has deliberately ignored the region, keeping it under its complete control and denying the people of Jammu and Kashmir, under its occupation, basic aviation travel facilities.

The Gilgit Airport has a modest infrastructure with a short runway, where only small aircraft like the ATR 42 can operate. The only civilian traffic the airstrip witnesses on a daily basis is the PIA-operated single flight to Islamabad. The Pakistani Airforce operates the airport and uses Lockheed C-130 Hercules for its own operations. The other operational airport in the region is Skardu International Airport. By name, the airport is international but has not witnessed any international flight till date. There are just two daily flights operated from the airport by PIA and Air Blue Islamabad. It has two asphalt runways of 11,944 ft (3,641 m) each. The airport doubles as the forward base for Pakistan Air Force in the region as PAF Base Qadri. During the 1971 Bangladesh War, the Indian Air Force (IAF) surprised the PAF by bombing the runway and other infrastructure at the base, which crippled Pakistan's air navigation from the Northern Areas.[24]

On the other hand, J&K has four airports to cater to its population and lakhs of tourists who visit it annually. These include *Sheikh Ul Alam* Srinagar International Airport, and three domestic airports at Jammu, Kargil and Leh. Of these, Srinagar Airport witnesses large air traffic, with the daily number of flights averaging around 80. The airport has an integrated terminal, handling both domestic and international flights. It covers 19,700 m^2 (212,000 sq ft) and can serve 950 passengers at a time: 500 domestic and 450 international passengers. It has a single asphalt runway and is equipped to handle an instrument landing system to address the issues arising from bad weather conditions and make it suitable for night-landing. The terminal building of the airport looks like the Himalayas and is laced with modern facilities and amenities like food courts, some Kashmiri handicraft shops, banking facilities, and foreign currency exchange outlets to smoothen passenger travel. Given Kashmir's all-year tourist inflow, the airport acts as an important mode of transportation for locals and tourists alike. In April 2022, the airport handled a record 102 flights in a day, flying over 15000 people in and out of Kashmir, which evidences how the infrastructure has improved over the years.[25] Likewise, Jammu airport and Leh Airport, respectively, on average, operate 50 and 15 flights daily.

The above statistics reflect the monumental disparity between the two regions of the state, with J&K writing its own developmental story in improving the aviation infrastructure in the state and providing the people with an all-around mode of air transportation medium. PoJK, on the other hand, with its near non-existent civil aviation infrastructure, especially with Muzaffarabad and Rawalakot airports non-operational status, continues denying the region's inhabitants a right to air travel. The residents of the PoJK are forced to travel through

Islamabad or Lahore airports for any foreign travel, ensuring the region remains cut off from the aviation map. This is even though nearly one and half million Kashmiris from PoJK are expatriate workers in Britain and Gulf majorly and send back remittances worth billions of dollars.

Modes of Communication

Telecommunication: The Government of Pakistan has entrusted Special Communications Organisation (SCO) to establish, run and maintain the telecom network across PoJK. This comes under the direct control of the Ministry of Information Technology and Telecommunications (MOITT). Its services include landline Telephone (PSTN), Mobile (GSM), Wireless Local Loop (WLL), Internet Broadband (DSL) and Digital Cross Connect (DXX). It has also laid over 2500 Kms of Optical Fiber Cable network in the region.[26] The Pakistani Government gave SCO a monopoly over all the services in the region, which in effect provided it with a means of controlling a single operator in the region as and when it intends to enforce an information blockade in the region in the face of anti-Pakistan protests on a regular basis by the Kashmiris. Though other operators were allowed inside PoJK following massive protests, the Government maintains tight control over the region's information.

On the other hand, Jammu and Kashmir has a vibrant telecommunication network, including mobile telephone, broadband, and Optical Fiber Cable network. Mobile phone communication was introduced in the state in 2003, and since then, it has witnessed exponential growth with teledensity at 86.08 per cent and the subscriber base at 12,082,518 by December 2021. J&K has around 140 thousand broadband subscribers in terms of wireline penetration. The major services providers include state-owned BSNL, along with Airtel, Jio, and Vodafone. In 2020, the state government launched J&K Communication and Connectivity Infrastructure Policy (JKCCIP) to ensure the smooth development and functioning of the telecommunications sector. Through this policy, the government aims to improve telecom and internet connectivity in the state to fulfil objectives under the National Broadband Mission, as applicable across the country.

Postal Network: Jammu and Kashmir have an extensive Postal network. Currently, it has 1695 post offices with its headquarters at Srinagar. In contrast, PoJK has a significantly low count of post offices, numbering 150, as highlighted below.

Power Infrastructure

Power Supply and Grid Networks: The installed grid

Table 2.4 Postal Network of J&K and PoJK

	J&K	PoJK
Post Offices	1695	150

Source: The date is sourced from the official websites of J&K, POJK ('AJK' and 'GB') government websites respectively.[27]

capacity in PoJK stands at 647.30 MVA. Of the 1771 villages, the PoJK government claims to have electrified 1764 villages, supplying roughly 3.616 million population with electricity, through a transmission lines network of about 30900 km. It represents 93 per cent of the PoJK population. The per capita electricity consumption in PoJK presently stands at around 403 kWh.[28] On the other hand, Pakistan Occupied Gilgit-Baltistan remains an isolated island and disconnected from the national grid network of Pakistan. Electricity is usually supplied overshot distances through 11kV distribution lines with small clusters augmented with 66kV transmission lines.[29]

Compared to PoJK, the electricity distribution across Jammu and Kashmir is undertaken through 220 kV and 132 kV transmission lines. It has 4250 MVA transmission grid capacity at 132 kV level and 5120.5 MVA grid capacity at 66-33 kV level. Electricity is supplied through 1,32,173.99 km Distribution Line Length across Jammu and Kashmir, of which HT Line Length comprises 26941 Km, and LT Line Length stands at 89,921 Kms.[30] The state boasts of a wide network of grid stations and local feeder stations, which lights every nook and corner of the state.

Power Generation: Power holds the key to any economic activity. The identified hydropower potential of PoJK is 9258.620 MW. The commissioned power projects presently generate 2362 MWs of electricity, of which the major share is contributed by the Mangla Dam raising Project (110 MW) and Neelum Jhelum Hydro-Electric Project (969MW). It has important what a tragedy the Mangla Dam has been since its inception. Conceived in the 1960s and inaugurated in 1967, the project submerged close to 280 villages in Mirpur district and forced out close to 1,10,000 Kashmiris from PoJK. Additionally, the government of Pakistan reneged on its initial commitments of exploiting the water resources of the state against a water royalty towards the PoJK government, which Islamabad never honoured and instead has taken control over the whole project, thereby denying the regional government a source of revenue it could have generated on account of selling the electricity on its own.

In the case of Gilgit-Baltistan, the local power production stands at 113 MW in summer and 86 MWs in winter, against the demands of 254 MW in summer and 452 MW in winter. There exists a shortfall of 141 MW in summer and 366 MW in winter.[31] This meagre production and supply of electricity to GB has forced people to rely on traditional means of energy, including firewood, LPG, and kerosene oil.[32] Despite the surplus power generation, the Pakistani government supplies PoJK, excluding Gilgit-Baltistan, with a meagre 300-330 MWs of electricity against its peak demand of 400 MWs.[33] In the case of Gilgit-Baltistan, the scenario is worse with its harsh winter conditions, which have kept the region dependent on coal and other fuels. Instead of supplying the surplus energy generated in PoJK across its regions, including GB, Islamabad continues to feed its provinces and deliberately keeps the residents of this occupied territory in darkness. This exposes how the Pakistani state keeps PoJK under darkness and engages in brazen resource theft as the Jammu Kashmir resources are stolen to sustain its provinces.

Compared to PoJK, the hydropower potential of Jammu and Kashmir is estimated at 20,000 MW, of which 16475 MW have been identified. This comprises 11283 MW in the Chenab basin, 3084 MW in the Jhelum basin, 500 MW in Ravi Basin and 1608 MW in the Indus basin.[34] However, only 1/5th of the identified potential has been exploited. This includes 1220 MW in the state sector, 2009 MW in the central sector and 42.5 MW in the private sector. To harness this natural resource to its full potential, in the state sector, the Government of Jammu and Kashmir and the Central Government entered into many agreements over time. This has seen the participation of the National Hydroelectric Power Corporation (NHPC), investing significant capital in building and commissioning several projects to increase the electricity generation in the state. Unlike PoJK, Jammu and Kashmir Government enters into agreements with the corporations like NHPC on its terms. These agreements usually entail the projects being built, run and handover (after a specific period to allow the investing companies to recover a share of their capital) to the state. This not only created the power infrastructure on the ground but has ensured that the state retains control over its resources. In J&K, the power generated during 2017-18 stood at 5278.57 million units under state sector power projects. The total power availability in 2017-18 stood at 21502.87 million units, which translates into per capita power availability for J&K as 365.839 kwhs (2016-17). The average power demand in the state hovers around 2400 MWs against the supply of 2061 MWs, with the shortfall usually procured from the market, depending on the availability in the energy market.

This explains how PoJK has been made to give in to the dictates of the Pakistani government and is denied control over their assets like the Mangla Dam. Pakistan's Water and Power Development Authority (WAPDA), which owns the project, even denies the state their agreed upon water royalty on account of the resource exploitation over the years to the tune of millions of dollars.

Drinking Water Supply

The PoJK governmental figures put the availability of piped water supply in urban areas at 82 per cent and the rural population at 44 per cent. Out of 1654 villages, only 1032 have access to a water supply facility. In Gilgit-Baltistan areas, the access to the piped water supply is below 40 per cent, even as snow and glacial water remain a principal water source. Though the glacial water is usually crystal clear, requiring little treatment to make it drinking standards, nevertheless, 4/5th (80 per cent) of the available drinking water has been found unsafe for human consumption, with just 22 per cent complying with the drinking water standards of WHO.[35] Likewise, the drinking water supplied in PoJK has been found to be unsafe.[36]

Compared to PoJK, Jammu and Kashmir has connected 54 per cent of households through piped water supply out of 1.817 million households by December 2020.[37] Under the flagship program of the Jal Jeevan Mission, the Jal Shakti Department of the Government aims to achieve 100 per cent coverage of the households by December 2022. It ambitiously implements Village Action Plans (VAPs) with respect to villages for source strengthening, supply, management, operation and management to ensure the piped connectivity is durable and safe.[38] In the 2020-21 reports of the NITI AAYOG, 99.89 per cent of the rural population in Jammu and Kashmir has access to improved drinking water sources, the most amongst any Indian state.[39]

Health Facilities

The healthcare infrastructure in PoJK presents an abysmal scenario like other primary developmental indicators. According to governmental statistics, around 2790 hospital beds are available in the occupied region, excluding GB, which averages one bed per 1523 people.[40] The region has approximately 23 hospitals, including six district-level hospitals. Furthermore, there are 11 Tehsil/Civil headquarter hospitals, 50 Rural Health Centers, 225 Basic Health Units, 79 dispensaries, and 201 Mother and Child Health Centers.[41] In terms of human resources, there are just 1066 doctors, of which 60 are Health Managers, 302 are specialists, and 79 are dental surgeons and the rest 704 as Medical Officers. This translates to the ratio of 0.07 Per 1000 Population with respect to healthcare specialists, 0.16 for Medical Officers and 0.09 for Dentist surgeons.[42] In Gilgit-Baltistan, there are around 499 health facilities, which are staffed by 248 medical officers and specialists.[43] This humble infrastructure aside, the region lacks any tertiary care health facilities, which forces the people to travel to other provinces and ensure their dependence on the outside.

On the other hand, the healthcare infrastructure in Jammu and Kashmir has made an extensive penetration across the region. The state boasts of an extensive network of 3834 healthcare facilities, including 22 district hospitals, 84 Community Health Centers (CHCs), 398 Primary Health Centers (PHCs), 239 New Type PHCS, 355 MAC, 1910 SC, and New SCs 826. Besides these, there are three major tertiary care hospitals and 11 medical colleges, including 2 All India level and their associated hospitals. The number of beds available in public health facilities is 11342. Besides Ministry of Defense runs 11 hospitals with a capacity of 2643 beds.[44] J&K, as such, has one bed per 1066 people, besides one doctor per 1180 people, which translates into 1.18 doctors per 1000 population. According to the Central Bureau of Health Intelligence (CBHI), 15559 allopathic doctors are registered in J&K. In addition, there are 5823 AYUSH doctors employed in J&K, apart from 4127 dental surgeons.

The most prominent hospitals in the state include Sher-i-Kashmir Institute of Medical Sciences, Srinagar, Shri Maharaja Hari Singh (SMHS) Hospital Srinagar, Shri Maharaja Gulab Singh (SMGS) Jammu, Lal Ded Maternity Hospital Srinagar, GB Pant Hospital Srinagar, Government Medical College Srinagar, Government Medical College Jammu, Acharya Shri Chander College of Medical Sciences and Hospital (ASCOMS) Jammu,

Chest Disease Hospital Srinagar, Bone and Joint Hospital Srinagar, etc.

Table 2.5 Key Health Indicators of J&K and PoJK

Indicator	J&K	PoJK	
		'AJK'	GB
Infant Mortality Rate (Per 1000 live births)	22	62	73.5
Under 5 Mortality Rate (per 1000 live births)	16	96	91.8
Maternal Mortality Ratio (per 100,000 live births)	46	201	450-500
EPI Coverage (all vaccines)	93 per cent	94 per cent	38.7 per cent
Facility-Based Delivery	85.6 per cent	51 per cent	42.6 per cent
Contraceptive Prevalence Rate	46 per cent	30 per cent	38.1 per cent
Total Fertility Rate	1.6	3.8	4.6
Life Expectancy at birth	74 years	67.3	68.1 years
Birth Rate (per 1000 inhabitants)	15.4	NA	46.9
Iodised Salt Use	99.8 per cent	15 per cent	68.4 per cent

Source: PSLM 2014-15, PDHS 2012-13, pwd.GilgitBaltistan.gov.pk/population profile, http://health.Gilgit-Baltistan.gov.pk, & Technical Resource Facility, Islamabad, Pakistan, Department of Health, Jammu and Kashmir

There is a gross mismatch between the health spending between these regions. Taking the budgetary allocations for the 2019-20-year, J&K spent roughly ten times more financial capital of around US$ 618 million against PoJK's mere US$ 62 million. This is reflected in the basic health indicators between these two regions. PoJK has a ratio of 0.07 Per 1000 Population with respect to healthcare specialists, which is way below J&K's ratio of 1.18 per 1000 population. Likewise, J&K scores over PoJK in terms of hospital beds with its one bed per 1066 people against the latter's one bed per 1523 persons. The Infant Mortality Rate (Per 1000 live births), as highlighted in the table below, of J&K is well three times less than PoJK.

The Under 5 Mortality Rate (per 1000 live births) presents a wider disparity of around six times better for J&K at 16 than PoJK at above 90. The facility-based delivery, that is, hospital-handled childbirth, also shows how J&K has improved its infrastructure for its residents, with over 85 per cent of the childbirths in health care facilities against PoJK's below 50 per cent. These only manifests how Pakistan has ensured that the region remains backward, and its inhabitants depend on travelling to other provinces of Pakistan to access health care facilities.

Education

As PoJK is managed by the Pakistani state through two administrative setups, most of the socio-economic indicators are therefore presented separately for these two units of 'AJK' and GB. The literacy in 'AJK' hovers around 77.5 per cent, with the male literacy rate at 87.8 per cent and female at 67.7 per cent. This is despite Enrollment at the Primary Level of around 90 per cent (95 per cent for boys and 88 per cent for girls). The education in PoJK is majorly a governmental affair. Though it allocates 28 per cent of its recurring budget to the education sector, it has proven insufficient to transform the physical infrastructure of the educational institutions to make their environment conducive to providing quality education.

Additionally, while the share of budgetary allocations of more than a quarter of the whole budget appears substantial, it should be noted that the total budgetary allocation of 'AJK' is just US$ 78.55 million (141 billion Pakistan rupees). In terms of Infrastructure, it has a network of 6697 educational institutions at the pre-college level. This includes 4127, 1003 middle schools, 746 high schools, and 103 higher secondary schools. Besides, there are 718 private educational institutions in the state.[45] As per the Annual Status of Education Report (ASER), 40 per cent of the school in PoJK function without any buildings. On average, 52 per cent of students study within one classroom that lack basic amenities. Furthermore, 87 per cent of the schools lack electricity, 73 per cent without the availability of drinking water, and 82 per cent without boundary walls. This results in the outcome of educational indicators being dismal.

Table 2.6 Education in J&K and PoJK			
Indicator	J&K	PoJK	
		'AJK'	GB
Literacy Rate	77.30 per cent	77.5 per cent	53 per cent
Male	85.70 per cent	87.8 per cent	66 per cent
Female	68 per cent	67.7 per cent	41 per cent

Source: The date is sourced from the official websites of J&K, POJK ('AJK' and 'GB') government websites respectively.[46]

In the higher education sector, there are six universities in PoJK. These include the University of Azad Jammu and Kashmir Muzaffarabad, Mirpur University of Science and Technology Mirpur, Mohi-ud-Din Islamic University at Trarkhal, University of Kotli, University of Poonch Rawalakot, Women University of Azad Jammu and Kashmir Kotli. The three medical colleges are Mohi-ud-Din Islamic Medical College, Mohtarma Benazir Bhutto Shaheed Medical College and Poonch Medical College.

The Gilgit-Baltistan region has comparatively a modest literacy rate of 53 per cent, which includes 66 per cent of male literacy and 41 per cent of female literacy. Its Primary Level Gross Enrollment Rate stands at 87 per cent. In terms of institutional infrastructure, the region has 3526 schools, of which 1671 function at the primary level, 554 at the middle level, 421 at the high school level, and 113 at the higher secondary level, besides 767 private schools at different levels. There are 7 Degree Colleges, 18 Inter Colleges and two universities in the higher education sector. The universities are Karakorum International University Gilgit and the University of Baltistan Skardu. The region lacks college-level institutions in medicine, engineering and IT domain.

The Scenario in J&K

On the other hand, Jammu and Kashmir state has made perceptible progress in the education sector by creating necessary infrastructure besides enhancement of enrolment, checking dropout rate, capacity building, addressing gender inequality etc. Over the years, the central government has extended a number of schemes like Sarva Shiksha Abhiyan, National Programme for Education of Girls at Elementary Education (NPEGEL), Mid–Day Meals in Schools and Kasturba Gandhi Balika Vidyalaya and other initiatives to J&K. These positive governmental interventions have resulted in the literacy rate increasing to 78 per cent by 2018, together with Gross Enrolment ratio.[47] Though a governmental affair for long, the education sector has seen phenomenal private sector participation, contributing to the overall transformation of the education scenario in the state. As far as the educational infrastructure is concerned, J&K has 28154 government-run schools, of which 14570 are primary schools, 7052 middle schools, 1276 high schools, and 712 higher secondary schools. Besides, there are around 5256 private schools at multiple levels. During the last few years, the J&K Government has introduced major changes in the education sector with path-breaking decisions to ensure quality, equity, accessibility, accountability and affordability. The Mid-Day Meal (MDM) Scheme has been extended across the state to improve the nutritional standing of school-age children. Furthermore, it has announced establishing around 500 Kindergartens in the existing government schools across the state to increase enrolment, provide early child care education and enhance numerical and foundational literacy. As a part of infrastructural development, the state has announced establishing 518 smart/virtual classrooms in higher secondary schools for imparting quality education to students, apart from 200 Vocational laboratories for imparting vocational/skill training.

In the higher education domain, the state has 142 government degree colleges, nine medical colleges, four dental colleges, ten engineering colleges, and 17 universities. Besides, there are around 210 private colleges which offer teacher education degrees. The universities are: University of Kashmir (UoK) Srinagar, University of Jammu (UoJ) Jammu, Central Sanskrit University-Shree Ranbir Campus at Jammu, Sher-e-Kashmir University of Agricultural Sciences and Technology (SKUAST)

Table 2.7 Comparative Analysis of the Scenario of education in J&K and PoJK			
Indicator	**J&K**	**PoJK**	
		'AJK'	**GB**
Primary	14570	4127	1671
Middle Schools	7052	1003	554
High Schools	1276	746	421
Higher Secondary Schools	712	103	113
Private schools	5256	718	767
Total No. of Schools	***28154***	***10223***	
Inter Colleges	NA	93	18
Degree Colleges	142	74	7
Post Graduate colleges	19	13	NA
Dental Colleges	4	0	NA
Medical Colleges	9	3	NA
Nursing Colleges	2	NA	NA
Engineering colleges	10	8	NA
Private colleges	208	NA	NA
Total No. of Colleges	***394***	***216***	
Universities	11	5	2

Source: The date is sourced from the official websites of J&K, POJK ('AJK' and 'GB') government websites respectively.[48]

Kashmir, Sher-i-Kashmir Institute of Medical Sciences (SKIMS) Srinagar, Sher-e-Kashmir University of Agricultural Sciences and Technology (SKUAST) Jammu State, Shri Mata Vaishno Devi University at Katra, Islamic University of Science and Technology (IUST) Awantipora, Pulwama, Baba Ghulam Shah Badhshah University (BGSBU) Rajouri, Central University of Jammu (CUJ) Samba, Central University of Kashmir (CUK) Ganderbal, Cluster University (CU) Jammu, Cluster University (CU) Srinagar.

Other institutions of importance are the National Institute of Technology (NIT) at Srinagar, Indian Institute of Mass Communication (IIMC) at Jammu, Indian Institute of Management (IIM) Jammu, Indian Institute ofTechnology (IIT) at Jammu, All India Institute of Medical Sciences (AIIMS) in Jammu, (AIIMS), Srinagar, National Institute of Fashion Technology (NIFT) Srinagar, Institute of Engineering Technology and Research (IETR) Jammu, and National Institute of Electronics and Information Technology (NIEIT) Jammu. Aside from earlier four medical colleges, the state government has set up five Medical Colleges, one each at Kathua, Doda, Rajouri, Baramulla and Anantnag, having 100 MBBS seats each.

The J&K government has also set up two schools of Architecture in the two provinces of the state. The government has also announced the setting up the first

Medical University in the state, which would manage the affairs of Medical Colleges, para-medical institutes, and dental colleges. This pervasive network of educational institutes has ensured that Jammu and Kashmir's Gross Enrollment Ratio (GER) at the Primary level reached 97.25 with Net Enrollment Ration (NER) at 87.30 and GER at 94.74 at the Upper Primary level with 82.12 NER.

In terms of educational spending in the two regions, J&K spent around US$ 1.55 Billion in 2020 against PoJK's mere US$ 173 million, despite being 28 per cent of its annual budget. Against the 8791 schools of different levels in PoJK, there are close to 22898 educational institutions in the state of Jammu and Kashmir by 2021. There are 11 universities in J&K against 7 in PoJK, whereas there are nine medical colleges, apart from two AIIMS against just three in the Pakistani-occupied territory of the state.

There is not a single Dental college in PoJK, which is an anomaly in itself. The people of PoJK have thereby very limited avenues to access higher education in the region and are majorly forced to travel to other Pakistani provinces. J&K has established two Schools of Architecture in the state.

Regarding the Teacher Student Ratio, J&K has definitely better indicators. Between the two units in PoJK, AJK is ahead of GB, which scores very low.

Table 2.8 Teacher Education Ratio in J&K and PoJK

Teacher Student Ratio (students per teacher)	J&K	PoJK	
		'AJK'	GB
Schools	15	16.5	35.8
Colleges	36	18.24	NA
Universities	NA	28.07	NA

Source: The date is sourced from the official websites of J&K, POJK ('AJK' and 'GB') government websites respectively.[49]

Poverty

The poverty line is used to measure poverty and the basis for identifying the poor. The state of J&K has a poverty ratio of 12.58 per cent against the national average of 26.5 per cent, as per the National Multidimensional Poverty Index (MPI) Baseline Report (2020) of NITI Aayog. This reflects how the state has arrested poverty despite continued externally induced disturbances over the decades. The central government has also extended its poverty alleviation programs like Indira Awas Yojna and other Below Poverty Line schemes to the state, which has helped the state to keep the poverty well below the national average. It created opportunities for poor people through the process of accelerated economic growth and expanding their asset base while enhancing security which is essential for poverty reduction. The Government of Jammu and Kashmir runs Jammu and Kashmir Rural Livelihood Mission (JKRLM), a state-wide poverty alleviation programme "to reduce poverty in the state by building strong grassroots institutions for the poor, engaging them in gainful livelihoods interventions and ensuring appreciable improvement in their income on a sustainable basis."[50] Through this, the State Government has established a robust mechanism to identify the poor population and extends its capital programs to earn a decent livelihood while putting safety nets around this vulnerable section through its welfare mechanism. This has helped set up 60,000 Self Help Groups (SHG) across the state, including extending benefits to 5, 02641 women. Clubbed with the Mission Youth programme, it has become a viable medium to help generate self-employment and help them move their families out of the poverty circle. The Government of India has also extended its poverty reduction programmes to the state to help bring this small section of the population out of economic distress. These include Pradhan Mantri SVANidhi Scheme, Integrated Rural Development Programme (IRDP), Pradhan Mantri Awas Yojana, Mahatma Gandhi National Rural Employment Guarantee Act (MGNREGA), National Food Security Act, National Rural Livelihoods Mission (NRLM), National Urban Livelihood Mission (NULM), Pradhan Mantri Jan-Dhan Yojana (PMJDY), Pradhan Mantri Kaushal Vikas Yojana (PMKVY), Prime Minister Jeevan Jyoti Bima Yojana, Pradhan Mantri Suraksha Bima Yojana, Prime Minister Ujjwala Plan, PM Garib Kalyan

Yojana (PMGKY), National Nutrition Mission – Poshan Abhiyan, and National Pension Scheme, among others.

In the case of PoJK, the poverty is overall twice as much as in J&K. According to a 2016 report by Pakistan's Ministry of PD&R and UNDP, 24.9 per cent of people in 'AJK', part of PoJK are multidimensionally poor, whereas, for Gilgit-Baltistan, it is 43 per cent. Overall, more than half the number of households in PoJK, numbering around 350 thousand households, are under the National Poverty Scorecard (NPS) of Pakistan, a stark reminder of the chronic poverty in the occupied territory of Pakistan. The Government of Pakistan has launched International Fund for Agricultural Development (IFAD) supported AJK Community Development Programme (AJKCDP) in PoJK "to improve the livelihoods and incomes of poor rural households with the institutionalisation of community-driven development within the government development framework through supporting capacity development of local institutions (community organisations (COs), village organisations (VOs) and local support organisations (LSOs)) to function and implement community-driven development plans."[51] However, the region continues to battle widescale poverty. This has resulted in close to 29 per cent of the population being undernourished, whereas 57.1 per cent of people are food insecure, with 25.9 per cent facing moderate to severe insecurity and 5.7 per cent being severely food insecure. In terms of nutrition, 31.7 per cent of children under the age of 5 are stunted compared to 43.7 per cent nationally. The proportion of underweight children is 25.8 per cent. These figures manifest a gross variance between J&K and PoJK, which goes on to establish how India has been able to intervene affirmatively in the state against Pakistan's colonial thinking of keeping the region dependent on begging for Islamabad's largesse. The poverty in the PoJK is chronic also because of the PoJK government's inability and unwillingness to undertake land reforms like the Pakistan government itself, which has continued nurturing the 19th-century feudality in the region. For any meaningful intervention to bring the region out of poverty, the PoJK Government would need to undertake land reforms (which is highly unlikely), and improve the deliverable services like access to clean drinking water, subsidised food and fuel, road infrastructure and public transportation system, and healthcare.

Unemployment

Pakistan's continued sponsorship of the militancy in J&K, inhibiting private investments into the state, has resulted in the governmental jobs being an important employment generation sector even as tourism, agriculture, and allied sectors contribute substantially. Considering these factors, the rate of unemployment in the state remains around 17 per cent, with the government taking comprehensive steps to tackle the unemployment problem by emphasising employment in the private sector, self-employment and skill development to enhance the employability of the youth.

The J&K government has established District Employment & Counselling Centers across every state district to dynamically and proactively approach dealing with the changing unemployment scenario at each level. To foster inclusive economic growth through the development of entrepreneurship culture in the state, the government has turned 1997-established the Jammu and Kashmir Entrepreneurship Development Institute (JKEDI) into a nodal agency for encouraging the youth into entrepreneurship. Its schemes primarily focus on providing sustainable livelihood opportunities to the educated unemployed youth of the state through guidance, mentorship, training and access to financial capital under various Government sponsored schemes. The J&K Government also launched the Mission Youth Programme, through which a number of skill development schemes have been launched to skill the youth and help them with livelihood opportunities. J&K also has a Self-Employment Scheme under which the Government extends "margin money, capital and interest subsidy assistance to the educated unemployed youth of the State for establishing their own employment generating units."[52] It further aims "to create maximum employment opportunities in Jammu and Kashmir and to solve the growing unemployment in rural areas, empower the youth, provide and support self-employment," and create an entrepreneurial ecosystem in J&K. The state also runs the J&K Rural Employment Generation Programme (JKREGP), under Khadi and Village Industries Board, to harness and divert the energy and enthusiasm of the youth of the state for the establishment of the productive enterprise in the micro industrial sector and to create employment opportunities in rural as well as urban areas of the state. It further mobilises the bank finance for establishing the Village Industries sector of the state on modern lines to help generate employment opportunities in rural areas of the state by setting up new self-employment ventures/projects/village industries enterprises. It extends financial credit to the youth to set up their industrial units in sectors like the Agro & Food Processing Industry, Handmade Paper/Fiber Products, Mineral Based Products, Polymer & Chemical Based Industry, Rural Engineering & Biotechnology, Service Industry, and Textiles. Apart from this, the Government of India has also extended a number of schemes to the state to help generate employment avenues for the youth.

On the other hand, the unemployment rate in PoJK hovers around 18.44 per cent. Youth unemployment has continued to rise owing to multiple factors, most significantly the absence of any comprehensive employment generation strategy in the region for the last 70 years.[53] It has been unable to implement a coherent and integrated Youth Employment Strategy like the J&K EDI initiative or Employment Counseling Centers to make any visible impact. These unemployment figures are high compared to J&K, where Pakistan has continued to create disturbances through the menace of militancy, which has hindered the inflow of major investments and set up a robust industrial base.

Overall Economic Condition

For the past 74 years, the Pakistani military establishment, in collaboration with Pakistani top bureaucracy, multinational corporations and now China, and with the cooperation of local facilitators in AJK and GB has been plundering the natural resources of what essentially are Indian territories which till this day remain under the illegal occupation of Pakistan. A brief survey of the scale of the pillage of the natural resources of GB by Pakistan would reveal the size and volume of the robbery.

Exploitation of PoJK Resources

Let us begin by examining the theft of the water resources flowing through J&K. Construction on the Upper Jhelum Canal in the state of J&K began in 1913 and was completed in 1916. Right up to the day when Indian subcontinent was partitioned in 1947, the British were paying the J&K state yearly '*abiyana*' or water revenue. However, since Pakistan occupied Indian territory of J&K in 1947, not a single paisa has ever been paid to the so-called 'AJK' government. In 1967, Mangla dam was constructed on the river Jhelum. By 1975, it has recovered the cost of the construction of the dam. According to a Kashmiri scholar, Dr Shabbir Chaudhary, by 2010, Mangla dam had produced 250 billion units of electricity but not a single paisa in revenue collected by Pakistan has ever been shared with the government of the occupied territory of 'AJK' and GB. Chaudhary informs that at the time of partition, the total land covered with forests in PoJK was estimated at 1.6 million acres which were 42 per cent of the total landmass. Today the forests of AJK have shrunk to less than 14 per cent. Prime trees are cut down vigorously by the timber mafia which in actuality is an extended arm of the Pakistani military. It takes almost 100 years for a tree of *Diyar* (*deodar*) to grow to a height of 200 feet. Once cut it sells for a whopping Rs 30 to Rs 36 lakhs in Gujranwala and Lahore and then resold at an even higher rate.

According to a conservative estimate, says Dr Chaudhary, 1.8 to 2 million trees are being cut down each year. This is one of the major reasons for the frequent occurrence of landslides and the large number of fatalities during the 2005 earthquake. PoJK is being looted of PKR 51 billion and PKR 84 crore annually due to the stealing of trees alone. Each year, PoJK produces PKR 3 billion worth of flowers and herbs of medicinal value. There are no records available to show if Pakistan has paid any revenue to the government of the so-called Azad Kashmir whatsoever in this regard. Pakistan based corporations are making a profit of one billion rupees each year out of flowers and herbs from 'AJK' alone. There are vast deposits of major and minor metallic and non-metallic minerals and precious stones in both the 'AJK' and GB. These include marble, coal, gravel, sand, Bauxite, Ruby, diamond, emerald and gold to mention a few. There is 21.5 thousand million tonne of coal deposits available in PoJK alone. Precious stones in Neelum valley are valued at $21.5 billion, reveals Dr Chaudhary. US$ 40 billion worth of precious stones have been extracted from these occupied territories so far. In the vicinity of the capital of PoJK, Muzaffarabad, there are 1594 million tonnes of coal and 250 lakh tonnes of Gypsum reserves. And the people of 'AJK' are being forced to live in poverty and in sub-human conditions. Long hours of load-shedding has totally destroyed the small industries of 'AJK.' Lack of clean drinking water is a major cause of illnesses like hepatitis and dysentery. There is a general lack of hospitals and universities and mud roads that become unusable during monsoon and wintery snow showers and lack of basic necessities has become a daily norm in the occupied territories. Majority of youth in PoJK are forced to live under duress in the Middle East and Europe just to earn a meagre wage to support their families back home. And on top of this, if someone raises a question regarding the brutal plunder of our natural resources, she/he is harassed by the Pakistani secret services and in some cases even murdered extra-judicially.

Gilgit-Baltistan area in PoJK is the most neglected, backward and poorest area in entire South Asia where 85 per cent of the people make their living on subsistence farming,[54] but the state data shows only 23 per cent of the population are living in poverty.[55] In this connection, a multi-party conference was organised in Gilgit on 6 June 2017 by Astore Supreme Council where the speakers held Islamabad responsible for keeping the people of Gilgit-Baltistan economically backward for the last seven decades. Moreover, heavy taxes have been imposed time and again through ordinances without providing basic fundamental rights, such as constitutional status to the region. Against the imposition of illegal taxation massive anti-government protests have been held in Gilgit-Baltistan on a number of occasions. In 2017, such protests brought the socioeconomic activities to a standstill as the traders observed strike for almost two months. The protest call was given jointly by G-B Markazi Anjuman-i-Tajran, lawyers and trade bodies, contractors, hotel and

Petrol Pump Association and GB Chamber of Commerce and Industry who declared the imposition of new taxes as illegal and tantamount to "murder of traders."[56]

There has been an increasing frequency of suicide incidents in the region. In Ghizer district alone over 300 youth, both boys and girls, committed suicides since 2000 (*The Nation*, 21 May 2017.) One major reason for committing the suicides is unemployment. Those who are educated either join the government services or the Northern Light Infantry (NLI).[57] Moreover, there is discrimination in the pay structure as well. The natives who join the civil services are paid 25 per cent less than those in deputation from Punjab.[58]

The region earns most of its revenue from tourism and minerals. Based on a survey report carried out by Australian Agency for International Development (AUAID) and Pakistan Mineral Development Corporation (PMDC) in 1995, it was estimated that there are 1,480 gold mines in this area out of which 123 contain superior quality to the gold mines in South Africa.[59] But the mining industry has not flourished. According to the Gilgit-Baltistan Metals Minerals and Gem Association (GBMMGA), this could be because the companies who were issued mining leases and exploration licenses have become powerful mafia, intent on "keeping the sector backward for their ulterior motive."[60]

Tourism Industry has also suffered a major setback

in Gilgit-Baltistan. One of the most beautiful places in the world, Gilgit-Baltistan is very popular among tourists both from Pakistan and abroad. Surrounded by the world's largest mountain ranges– Hindukush to the Karakoram in the northeast with western Himalayas in the south and Pamir in the extreme north, Gilgit-Baltistan borders the Chinese province of Xinjiang to the north, Jammu and Kashmir to the east, 'AJK' to the south, Afghanistan and Central Asia, through the Wakhan Corridor to the northwest and Pakistan's Khyber Pakhtunkhwa to the west. The region covers 32 snow-clad peaks and narrow valleys–18,000 to 26,000 feet high–including the world's second-highest peak, K-2 or Chigori and the third-highest peak, Nanga Parbat. Gilgit-Baltistan is home to snow-clad mountains, mighty glaciers, lush green valleys and freshwater lakes.

Eighty per cent of foreign tourists coming to Pakistan visit Gilgit-Baltistan. However, the tourism industry, which was the only major source of employment, has suffered badly in recent years, particularly after Pakistan witnessed the rise in sectarian and militant violence that got exaggerated after 9/11 terror attacks, earthquakes and floods that have ravaged the area and the brutal killing of nine foreign tourists (five Ukrainians, three Chinese, one Russian and a local guide) by militants at Nanga Parbat on June 23, 2013. In the immediate aftermath, the inflow of foreign tourists came down by more than half, as only

4,524 foreign tourists visited Gilgit-Baltistan in 2013 as against 10,338 in 2007.[61] From the next year onwards, with improvement in security situation in Gilgit-Baltistan, the tourism industry witnessed an upward trend. According to Mubashir Ayub, Assistant Director, Gilgit-Baltistan Tourism Department, in 2017, around 1.72 million tourists visited GB. The revival of tourism industry brought revenue worth PKR 300 million to the local economy and it had a potential to generate local business worth PKR one billion according to media reports.[62] As much of it would depend on the security situation in the region, the GB government has decided to put curbs on public demonstrations and protests.[63] However, such highhandedness may backfire in future because it deprives people of the right to peaceful protests and holding rallies.

Economic Conditions in Jammu and Kashmir

The major contribution to the economy of J&K comes from exports; a substantial part of that comes from agriculture and allied activities, which are partially taxed. So, it does not have a robust tax base and results in dependence on the Centre for funds. The argument that the region's economy is dependent on the Centre, however, has to be understood in the right context. The erstwhile state was given the Special Category State status because the region is situated in the mountains and has difficult terrain as it is strategically situated along the borders of neighbouring countries. In the larger political economy perspective, there is a fostered dependence, which over the years has become a part of the system. As a result, the regional government was not obliged to raise resources to fund itself. This could be to keep the regional government in control.

Jammu and Kashmir has a population of roughly 1.25 crore. Following are the five major sectors contributing to the region's economy: agriculture and horticulture, tourism, handicrafts, industries and government jobs. About 65 to 70 per cent of Kashmir's population is supported by agriculture and horticulture. Although the service sector contributes around 50 per cent to the Union Territory's GDP, this sector employs a significant proportion of the population. The second sector is tourism, which varies but on average employs about a million people. The third is handicrafts, or the artisanal sector, which employs around 1 million people. The handicraft sector plays an important role in the state's economic structure, and its high-quality craftsmanship, appealing designs, and functional utility have earned it international renown. Fourth is the industry sector, which is in its early stages of development. About 5 lakh people are employed by the government. Apples and shawls were two goods that helped the economy withstand the militancy.

The economy of Kashmir valley is predominantly agricultural, with over 70 per cent population depending on it and allied activities. Within the agriculture sector, it is the horticulture sector that has gained prominence. Estimates suggest that the annual turnover of this sector is over Rs. 9,000 crores. The horticultural industry is crucial to Kashmir's economy, employing 700,000 households or 3.5 million people directly or indirectly.[64] The Valley is the country's largest apple grower. The Shopian district is known as the Country's apple bowl, with apple orchards covering 21,676 hectares. Saffron is another vital component of Kashmir's economy grown in three districts of Kashmir: Pulwama, Budgam, and Srinagar. Pampore in Pulwama has been crowned with the "saffron town" title since it produces the most and best quality saffron in the region. About 30,000 families in Pampore are associated with saffron cultivation.[65]

Tourism is also an important component of Kashmir's economy, accounting for 8 per cent of the UT's total GDP. According to industry estimates, this sector employs approximately 100,000 people directly and indirectly.[66] But this sector is very sensitive to the political situation in the Union Territory. The erstwhile state received 1,299,112 (1.29 million) tourists in 2016.[67] As per government records, numbers have been declining since, beginning with the long chain of violence following the killing of Burhan Wani. In February this year, the government acknowledged in the Parliament that post-removal of special status, tourism has been on the decline and only 84,000 tourists have visited Kashmir valley since 5 August 2019." The impact was felt more severely in Kashmir valley than in Jammu division," Union Tourism Minister Prahlad Patel told the Rajya Sabha.[68]

Though the economy of Jammu and Kashmir has been thriving, an important variable for economic growth is stability viz. political and institutional stability. If one looks at how Kashmir's economy has done in the last 20 years, one realises that the only periods of growth in the region's economy have been when there was reasonable political certainty and stability and a decline in violence. The bottom line is peace. Peace has to be ensured by people who are going to benefit out of it. People of the region should contribute towards strengthening and consolidating peace. It is the responsibility of the Central and UT governments to address all the issues that affect peace; eventually, prosperity follows peace.

Pakistan's Relationship with PoJK: A Tale of Exploitation and Oppression

The relationship of Pakistan with PoJK is that of a master and slave. Pakistan dictates terms to PoJK leadership and they are forced to follow accordingly. For illustration, the China-Pakistan Economic Corridor (CPEC), if it fully materialises, is believed to be a game changer for

Pakistan's economy. The CPEC is part of the ambitious Chinese Silk Road initiative, more widely known as 'One Belt One Road (OBOR)' or 'Belt and Road Initiative (BRI)', connecting Kashgar in Xinjiang with Gwadar Port in Pakistan. The relationship between Communist China and the Islamic Republic of Pakistan is a fine example of intricate interplay of geo-strategic and geo-economic aspirations of two countries in the region.

The launch of a major investment drive under the CPEC has helped Gilgit- Baltistan to acquire the status of a gateway to Central Asia. Although it would be premature to predict how much the CPEC benefits Gilgit-Baltistan; nonetheless, the region might gain some infrastructure in terms of roads and rail services. However, not much is being expected by the people of the region partly because the federal government hasn't announced any special economic zones (SEZs) in the region. All other provinces through which the Corridor is passing are getting SEZs, except Gilgit-Baltistan.[69] An editorial in a leading daily of Gilgit-Baltistan concludes thus, "Any confrontation by Gilgit-Baltistan would snap the trade ties between the two countries. The tragedy is that Pakistan has always been keen on signing agreements with China but it has deliberately kept Gilgit-Baltistan ignorant of all these developments! In accomplishing mega economic projects, Pak-China highway, and other projects, road goes through Gilgit-Baltistan."[70] The leadership of Gilgit-Baltistan has never been consulted on CPEC. That is not the case even with the restive provinces of Pakistan that are part of the Corridor, who have at least some say in its policy development. For example, when the federal government wanted to change the route of the Corridor, the leaders from Khyber-Pakhtunkhwa (KP) and Balochistan protested and forced the government to initiate work on the western route. The route from Gwadar to Kashghar was initially planned to pass through Bisima, Khuzdar, Kalat and Quetta, Zhob, Dera Ismail Khan, Hassan Abdal and onwards to Kashghar. However, the route was reportedly changed from Bisima, through Ratodero towards Punjab bypassing the risk-prone Baloch and Pakhtun areas. This highhanded approach of the Punjab-dominated federal government could simmer the already existing alienation against the Punjab province and affect the CPEC.[71] Nonetheless, after months of wrangling, the then PML-N government called an All Parties Conference (APC) in order to address the grievances of KP and Baluchistan regarding the corridor. A consensus was reached, and the political leaders from KP and Baluchistan were successful in persuading the Nawaz Sharif government to show flexibility and give in to the demands of other parties.[72]

However, such a case is not possible for the leadership of Gilgit-Baltistan: first, they do not have representation in the National Assembly; second, Islamabad does not take them seriously. As an editorial in a Gilgit-Baltistan daily puts it:

> At the end of the APC, all the political leaders went home happily as their reservations had been met by the federal government. But unfortunately no one even bothered to ask the people of Gilgit-Baltistan if they had any China-Pakistan Economic Corridor and Gilgit-Baltistan 205 reservations about the CPEC as it would pass through over 400 kilometres land in their area. The government did not bother to take the people of the region on board about the project. It also showed that the people having no representation in power corridors and deprived of their basic rights have no avenue to go to when they are discriminated against. Same has been done with the people of Gilgit-Baltistan for seven decades.[73]

While commenting on the growing presence of China in Gilgit-Baltistan, Senge Hasnan Sering, who heads the Institute of Gilgit-Baltistan Studies in Washington and is a vocal advocate of Gilgit-Baltistan's independence, claimed, "All the mining sites in the region were given to Chinese companies who are strengthening their bases there."[74] He further argued that constitutionally Gilgit-Baltistan is not a part of Pakistan, however, "it (Pakistan) just exploits our resources and wants to continue with its political hegemony. Even the latest empowerment package is a farce as the power centre continues to be in Pakistan."[75]

It is also believed that with the extension of the KKH, the Pakistani Government has decided to shift the dry port which was to be built up in Sost in Gilgit-Baltistan to Havelian in Hazara division of KP, which would have rendered thousands of people from Gilgit-Baltistan jobless.[76] Reacting to the relocation of the dry port, former president of the Chamber of Commerce and Industry, Javed Hussaini, said, "Livelihood of thousands of families of Gilgit-Baltistan is linked with the Sost dry port and it would be an economic disaster for them if existing activities are shifted to the newly proposed dry port at Havelian."[77] In the same vein, the former speaker of Gilgit-Baltistan Legislative Assembly, Wazir Baig said, "We are not clear about the benefits of the CPEC we will get, but we are much certain about the adverse effects due to relocation of the dry port."[78] The Federal government has verbally assured Gilgit-Baltistan of establishing two SEZs to compensate the people of the region, but nothing concrete has emerged in writing. The mainstream political parties of Gilgit-Baltistan have ostensibly supported the Corridor, but at the same time, expressed their reservations about the progress and benefits for the region. Jhanzaib Yaseen, a leader of the Gilgit-Baltistan chapter of the Pakistan Tehreek-i-Insaf (PTI), said that if economic zones are not established in the region, the CPEC is meaningless for the people of the Gilgit-Baltistan, adding that the CPEC will only benefit Punjab, and Gilgit-Baltistan will only get cheap labour and dust.[79] Moreover, Pakistan has been exploiting the scope of uranium enrichment in Pakistan-occupied Gilgit-Baltistan, confirmed locals and political activists from the occupied region. Sources in Gilgit-Baltistan said a team of Pakistani experts from the Atomic Energy Material Centre (AEMC) had visited the Haider Abad area of Hunza Nagar, Skardu and Ghizer areas of Gilgit-Baltistan.[80] They also visited an enrichment site located near the Dargai village in Malakand district of Khyber Pakhtunkhwa province for uranium exploration. Earlier, there were reports that Pakistan has given a free hand to Chinese mining companies to plunder natural resources in Gilgit-Baltistan. There are reports that over 2,000 leases for mining of gold, uranium and molybdenum have been illegally awarded to Chinese firms by the Pakistan government in occupied Gilgit-Baltistan and Khyber Pakhtunkhwa.

Concluding Observations

In light of the above data and facts, it can be well said that Jammu and Kashmir is more developed than PoJK. Since 1947, there has been constant progress in Jammu and Kashmir, but no improvement has occurred yet in PoJK. Moreover, the control of Pakistan over the resources of PoJK is immense, but the people of PoJK are bereft of the benefits of resources. They undergo continuous protests and have immense discontent for Pakistan in the occupied region. There are no democratic rights for the people in PoJK, while in Jammu and Kashmir, people exercise their democratic rights freely.

Moreover, Pakistan has been trying everything to incorporate Kashmir into its territorial borders, and this was a fundamental premise of the 'Two Nation Theory' that forms the ideological foundation upon which Pakistan as a state principally rests. Pakistan envisages Kashmir as a vital part of its territoriality. It continues to perceive itself as an incomplete Muslim state denied strategic depth without the accession of Kashmir to its territorial boundaries. Pakistan's imagining of a Muslim mother state would remain incomplete unless the state of Jammu and Kashmir accedes to it. The Pakistani state has nurtured a menagerie of non-state actors to achieve this. On the other hand, for India, Kashmir has been a symbol of secular nationalism, and it fears that its project of building a secular nation would receive an irretrievable setback if it lost Kashmir. The clash between India and Pakistan over Kashmir has resulted in the loss of many innocent lives. Pakistan has been hell-bent, right from the beginning, on incorporating Kashmir into its territory. While as India has been firm in its commitment to democratic principles and is eager to resolve the Kashmir issue as per the wishes of the people of Jammu and Kashmir. Overall, the data reflects that Jammu and Kashmir is far better than PoJK in almost all the developmental indicators. For illustration, J&K is twice richer than PoJK.

Similarly, J&K has 28154 schools and 394 Colleges compared to 10223 schools and 216 Colleges in PoJK. In other parameters, J&K is far ahead of PoJK, showcasing Pakistan's abysmal attitude towards PoJK. Even the healthcare scenario in PoJK lies in shambles. They have 23 hospitals, including six district-level hospitals, 11 Tehsil/Civil headquarters hospitals, 50 Rural Health Centers, 225 Basic Health Units, 79 dispensaries, and 201 Mother and Child Health Centers.

However, in J&K, there is an extensive network of 3834 healthcare facilities, including 22 district hospitals, 84 Community Health Centers (CHCs), 398 Primary Health Centers (PHCs), 239 New Type PHCS, 355 MAC, 1910 SC, and New SCs 826. This indicates a vast difference between J&K and PoJK in terms of development parameters. The data suggest that Pakistan has spread only lies and fabrications about the development of PoJK. They have done no substantial work in PoJK and left it high and dry. Every institution of PoJK is underdeveloped. While India, in Jammu and Kashmir, is continuously initiating developmental projects and building institutions for the common people.

On the other hand, in collaboration with China, Pakistan is plundering the natural resources of PoJK and pushing it further into the quagmire of poverty. The bogey of development which Pakistan is hypocritically portraying in PoJK is nothing but a façade. The above data explicitly reflects that India is building J&K while Pakistan is doing nothing to develop PoJK.

End Notes

1 For 'AJK' refer to https://www.ajk.gov.pk/, and for 'GB' refer to https://www.cmgb.gov.pk/

2 For J&K refer to https://jk.gov.in/.

3 Zulfikar Majid (2021), "J&K horticulture generates Rs 10,000 crore revenue annually," *Deccan Herald*, 6 October 2021, URL: https://www.deccanherald.com/national/north-and-central/jk-horticulture-generates-rs-10000-crore-revenue-annually-1037855.html

4 Jammu & Kashmir Official Portal, "Economy," URL: https://jk.gov.in/jammukashmir/?q=economy#:~:text=Jammu%20and%20Kashmir's%20economy%20is,popularly%20known%20as%20Kashmir%20Willow.

5 For J&K refer to https://jk.gov.in/, for 'AJK' refer to https://www.ajk.gov.pk/, and for 'GB' refer to https://www.cmgb.gov.pk/

6 "J&K horticulture generates Rs 10,000 crore revenue annually," URL: https://www.deccanherald.com/national/north-and-central/jk-horticulture-generates-rs-10000-crore-revenue-annually-1037855.html

7 Azad Jammu and Kashmir Agriculture Policy A Ten Years Perspective, URL: https://www.academia.edu/35438817/AZAD_JAMMU_AND_KASHMIR_AGRICULTURE_POLICY_A_Ten_Years_Perspective

8 Ishba Aziz Khan, "Growing Tourism in Azad Kashmir," Centre for Peace, Development and Reforms (CPDR), URL:http://www.cpdr.org.pk/index.php?option=com_content&view=article&id=704:growing-tourism-in-azad-kashmir&catid=113&Itemid=471

9 Ibid.

10 Rehmat Karim et al. (2021), "Estimating the Economic Contributions of Tourism Sector by Using Tourism Satellite Account (TSA) in Hunza-Nager District of Gilgit Baltistan-Pakistan," *International Journal of Scientific and Technology Research*, 10 (2): 216-229, URL: http://www.ijstr.org/finalprint/feb2021/Estimating-The-Economic-Contributions-Of-Tourism-Sector-By-Using-Tourism-Satellite-Account-tsa-In-Hunza-nager-District-Of-Gilgit-Baltistan-pakistan.pdf

11 Gilgit-Baltistan Government, "Tourism," URL: https://gilgitbaltistan.gov.pk/system/files?file=Tourism.pdf

12 Geo News (2021), "Gilgit Baltistan sees boost in tourism as 700,000 people visit region since May," July 26, 2021, URL: https://www.geo.tv/latest/361710-tourism-revives-as-up-to-700000-tourists-visit-gb-since-eid-ul-fitr

13 Gilgit-Baltistan Government, "Tourism," URL: https://gilgitbaltistan.gov.pk/system/files?file=Tourism.pdf

14 CEICDATA, "Visitor Arrivals: Local: Jammu and Kashmir," URL: https://www.ceicdata.com/en/india/resident-visits-by-states/visitor-arrivals-local-jammu--kashmir

15 M Saleem Pandit, "Jammu and Kashmir witnessing golden period of tourism, 80 lakh visited in past few months: LG," *The Times of India*, April 10, 2022, accessed at URL: https://timesofindia.indiatimes.com/india/jammu-and-kashmir-witnessing-golden-period-of-tourism-80-lakh-visited-in-past-few-months-lg/articleshow/90752262.cms

16 Department of Fisheries, J&K Government, URL: http://jkfisheries.in/

17 Ibid.

18 SH Baba et al. (2019), "Growth of fisheries sector in Jammu & Kashmir," *Journal of Pharmacognosy and Phytochemistry*, 8(4): 909-912.

19 Government of AJK, "Forestery and Fishries," accessed May 10, 2022, at URL: https://pndajk.gov.pk/ADP/2014-2015/Forestry%20Fisheries.pdf

20 "Jammu and Kashmir: The State Profile," *PHD Chamber of Commerce and Industry,* accessed May 15, 2022 at URL: http://phdcci.in/file/state%20profie_pdf/J&K-The%20 State%20Profile.pdf

21 IBEF, "Jammu and Kashmir Presentation and Economic Growth Report," accessed May 15, 2022 at URL: https://www.ibef.org/states/jammu-and-kashmir-presentation

22 CEICDATA, "Length of Roads: Jammu and Kashmir," accessed May 30, 2022 at URL: https://www.ceicdata.com/en/india/roads-and-highways-statistics-length-of-roads-by-state/length-of-roads-jammu-and-kashmir

23 Government of India Ministry of Road Transport and Highways, "Pragati Ki Nayi Gati," accessed May 15, 2022 at URL: https://morth.nic.in/sites/default/files/PragatiKiNayiGati/pdf/jammuandkashmir.pdf

24 India Today (2020), "How India pulverised Skardu airbase runway in PoK in 1971 war," URL: https://www.indiatoday.in/india/story/how-india-pulverised-skardu-airbase-runway-in-pok-in-1971-war-1747163-2020-12-06

25 The Economic Times (2022), "Srinagar airport registers record single-day flights, passengers," accessed May 30, 2022 at URL: https://economictimes.indiatimes.com/industry/transportation/airlines-/-aviation/srinagar-airport-registers-record-single-day-flights-passengers/articleshow/90801841.cms

26 Special communication Organisation (SCO), "Azad Jammu and Kashmir," accessed May 28, 2022 at https://

sco.gov.pk/Aboutus/aboutus.html

27 For J&K refer to https://jk.gov.in/, for 'AJK' refer to https://www.ajk.gov.pk/, and for 'GB' refer to https://www.cmgb.gov.pk/

28 Azad Jammu & Kashmir State Planning and Development Department, "Power Sector," accessed May 28, 2022 at URL: https://www.pndajk.gov.pk/majordevprojects.php?mid=4

29 Mazhar Ali et al (2021), "Techno-economic assessment and sustainability impact of hybrid energy systems in Gilgit-Baltistan, Pakistan," *Elsevier,* 7: 2546-2562, URL: https://www.sciencedirect.com/science/article/pii/S2352484721002523

30 Government of Jammu and Kashmir, "Power Development Department," accessed June 30, 2022 at URL: https://pdd.jk.gov.in/#

31 Energy Central (2019), "GB grid station phase-I to be completed at cost of Rs 5bln to overcome load shedding," 14 November 2019, URL: https://energycentral.com/news/gb-grid-station-phase-i-be-completed-cost-rs-5bln-overcome-load-shedding

32 Mazhar Ali et al (2021), "Techno-economic assessment and sustainability impact of hybrid energy systems in Gilgit-Baltistan, Pakistan," *Elsevier,* 7: 2546-2562, URL: https://www.sciencedirect.com/science/article/pii/S2352484721002523

33 Azad Jammu & Kashmir State Planning and Development

Department, "Power Sector," URL: https://www.pndajk.gov.pk/majordevprojects.php?mid=4

34 Government of Jammu and Kashmir, "Power Development Department," accessed May 30, 2022 at URL: https://pdd.jk.gov.in/#

35 Peer Muhammad (2014), "Gilgit-Baltistan waters run polluted," *The Third Pole*, 13 August 2014, URL: https://www.thethirdpole.net/en/pollution/gilgit-baltistan-waters-run-polluted/

36 Usman Ali et al. (2019), "Assessment of heavy metal contamination in the drinking water of Muzaffarabad, Azad Jammu and Kashmir, Pakistan," International Journal of Hydrology, 3 (5): 331-337, accessed May 30, 2022 at URL: https://medcraveonline.com/IJH/assessment-of-heavy-metal-contamination-in-the-drinking-water-of-muzaffarabad-azad-jammu-and-kashmir-pakistan.html

37 Jal Shakti Department, "Jal Jeevan Mission (JJM)," accessed May 30, 2022 at URL: https://jkjalshakti.nic.in/jjm.html

38 Deccan Herald (2020), "J&K plans to provide 100% tap water connections to rural households under JJM by Dec 2022," October 24, 2020, URL: https://www.deccanherald.com/national/north-and-central/jk-plans-to-provide-100-tap-water-connections-to-rural-households-under-jjm-by-dec-2022-906476.html

39 Anando Bhakto (2021), "NITI Aayog's SDG Index 2020-21: Only 53 per cent of the rural population in Jammu and

Kashmir has access to safe drinking water," *Frontline,* June 8, 2021, URL: https://frontline.thehindu.com/dispatches/niti-aayogs-sdg-index-2020-21-only-53-per-cent-of-the-rural-population-in-jammu-and-kashmir-has-access-to-safe-drinking-water/article34759458.ece

40 Health Department AJ&K, "Health Demography and Indicators," accessed May 30, 2022 URL: https://health.ajk.gov.pk/about#:~:text=Health%20coverage%20in%20Azad%20Jammu,Surgeons%2C%20and%20704%20Medical%20Officers.

41 Pakistan Health Knowledge Hub, "Azad Jammu and Kashmir: Regional RMNCAH&N Implementation Strategy and Action Plan (2016-2020)," accessed June 30, 2022 at URL: https://phkh.nhsrc.pk/sites/default/files/2019-06/AJK%20RMNCAH%26N%20Strategy%20 2016-2020.pdf

42 Health Department AJ&K, "Health Demography and Indicators," accessed May 30, 2022 URL: https://health.ajk.gov.pk/about#:~:text=Health%20coverage%20in%20Azad%20Jammu,Surgeons%2C%20and%20704%20Medical%20Officers.

43 Pakistan Health Knowledge Hub, "Gilgit Baltistan: Regional RMNCAH&N Implementation Strategy and Action Plan (2016-2020)," accessed June 30, 2022 at URL: https://phkh.nhsrc.pk/sites/default/files/2019-06/GB%20RMNCAH%26N%20Strategy%202016-2020.pdf

44 Ministry of Health and Family Welfare, "Hospitals in the

Country," July 24, 2018, accessed at URL: https://pib.gov.in/PressReleasePage.aspx?PRID=1539877

45 Azad Jammu and Kashmir Board of Intermediate Secondary Education Mirpur, accessed May 30, 2022 at URL: https://ajkbise.net/notifications/959716broucher201605onlyPrivateSchoolList.pdf

46 For J&K refer to https://jk.gov.in/, for 'AJK' refer to https://www.ajk.gov.pk/, and for 'GB' refer to https://www.cmgb.gov.pk/

47 Zulfikar Majid (2020), "Jammu and Kashmir's female literacy rate lower than all-India level, *Deccan Herald,* 19 September 2020, URL: https://www.deccanherald.com/national/north-and-central/jammu-and-kashmir-s-female-literacy-rate-lower-than-all-india-level-889762.html

48 For J&K refer to https://jk.gov.in/, for 'AJK' refer to https://www.ajk.gov.pk/, and for 'GB' refer to https://www.cmgb.gov.pk/

49 For J&K refer to https://jk.gov.in/, for 'AJK' refer to https://www.ajk.gov.pk/, and for 'GB' refer to https://www.cmgb.gov.pk/

50 "JKRLM Creates 60,000 SHGs With Over 5 Lakh Women Beneficiaries," *Kashmir Observer*, April 19, 2022, URL: https://kashmirobserver.net/2022/04/19/jkrlm-creates-60000-shgs-with-over-5-lakh-women-beneficiaries/

51 International Fund for Agricultural Development (IFAD), "AJK Community Development Programme – II (AJKCDP2)," accessed June 25, 2022 at URL: https://

www.ifad.org/en/-/document/ajk-community-development-programme-ii-ajkcdp2-

52 "J&K Self Employment Scheme," accessed June 20, 2022 at URL: http://www.jkslbc.com/jkses.php

53 ILO, "The Government of Azad Jammu and Kashmir to develop Youth Employment Strategy in collaboration with Prime Minister's Youth Programme and ILO," accessed June 20, 2022 at URL: https://www.ilo.org/islamabad/info/public/pr/WCMS_614732/lang--en/index.htm

54 Muhammad Amir Rana and Mujtaba Rathore, *Northern Areas: Crisis and Prospects, Pakistan Institute for Peace Studies*, Lahore, 2007, p. 56.

55 "Gilgit-Baltistan at a Glance 2013," accessed April 30, 2022 at www.gilgitbaltistan.gov.pk/DownloadFiles/GBFinancilCurve

56 Shabbir Mir (2018), "Unfair Tax Imposition in G-B," *The Express Tribune*, January 2, 2018, at https://tribune.com.pk/story/1598123/unfair-tax-imposition-g-b

57 The Northern Light Infantry, which was picked up for the task of intrusion of heights of Kargil, comprises special troops, trained in anti-heliborne, commando operations and snow warfare. Some of these soldiers are sent on deputation to the Special Service Group (SSG). See: Indian Defence Review, 14 (3), July-September 1999.

58 Shafqat Inqalabi, "Economic exploitation of Gilgit-Baltistan", in Virendra Gupta and Alok Bansal (eds.), *Pakistan Occupied Kashmir: The Untold Story*, p. 192.

59 Muhammad Amir Rana and Mujtaba Rathore, *Northern Areas: Crisis and Prospects*, 2007, p. 57

60 Raees Kamil (2011), "Real Threat to Mineral Industry in Gilgit-Baltistan," *Gilgit-Baltistan Times*, accessed May 30, 2022 at http://gbtimes.wordpress.com/2011/07/20/opinion-real-threat-to-mineralindustry-in-gilgit-baltistan/

61 Gilgit-Baltistan at a Glance 2013

62 Pamir Times (2017), "Record 1.72 million tourists visit Gilgit-Baltistan in past 11 months," accessed May 30, 2022 at http://http://pamirtimes.net/2017/11/29/1-72-million-tourists-visit-gilgitbaltistan/)

63 The Nation (2017), "Gilgit-Baltistan government to boost tourism," accessed May 30, 2022 at http:// nation.com.pk/28-apr 2017/gilgit-baltistan-government-to boost-tourism

64 Peerzada Ashiq (2018), "The apple of Kashmir's eye," *The Hindu*, accessed May 30, 2022 at https://www.thehindu.com/news/national/the-apple-of-kashmirs-eye/article22530623.ece

65 Safina Nabi (2020), "Government intervention has failed to arrest the decline of saffron cultivation in Kashmir," *Scroll*, accessed on May 18, 2022 at https://scroll.in/article/977579/government-intervention-has-failed-to-arrest-the-decline-of-saffron-cultivation-in-kashmir

66 Mir Ehsan and Ramesh Vinayak (2020), "Kashmir poised for a saffron surge," *The Hindustan Times*, accessed May 25, 2022 at https://www.hindustantimes.com/

india-news/kashmir-poised-for-a-saffron-surge/story-6Lkfur36bLOnMX2D3UcX4H.html

67 Athar Parvaiz (2017), "Thousands lose jobs as restive Kashmir's tourism economy dwindles," *The Hindustan Times*, accessed May 30, 2022 at https://www.hindustantimes.com/india-news/thousands-lose-jobs-as-restive-kashmir-s-tourism-economy-dwindles/story-n0C6bt8FiyurKP7JFHP8uN.html

68 Ibid.

69 For details on SEZ, see: Ministry of Planning Commission of Pakistan's report, *China-Pakistan Economic Corridor: Investment & Business Prospects*, August 2015, at http://202.83.172.247:8080/Complaints/China%20Pakistan%20Economic%Corridor%20%28

70 Daily Bang-e-Sehar (2014), "Nawaz Sharif's Visit to China and Gilgit-Baltistan," accessed May 30, 2022 at http://www.bangsehar.net//popoup.php?date=11-03-2014

71 Syed Ali Shah (2015), "Economic Corridor: ANP Denounces Change in Route, Calls APC," *Dawn*, accessed May 30, 2022 at www.dawn.com/news/1179361.

72 Abdul Manan (2015), "APC Consensus: Parties Settle on Corridor Route," *The Express Tribune*, accessed May 29, 2022 at http://www.tribune.com.pk/story/894068/apc-consensus-parties-settle-on-corridor-route/.

73 Daily Bang-e-Sahar (2015), "CPEC, Where Does Gilgit-Baltistan Stand?" accessed June 3, 20122 at http:// www.bangesahar.net/popup.php?lang=en&r_date=06-03-

2015&story=06-03-2015page-1-5.

74 Hakeem Irfan (2012), "Kashmiri Activists Seek India's Support to 'Save' PoK' from China's Increasing Strength," *Mail Online India*, accessed June 22, 2022 at http://www.dailymail.co.uk/indiahome/indianews/article-2105531.

75 Ibid

76 Peer Muhammad (2015), "CPEC to Cause Unemployment in Gilgit-Baltistan," *The Express Tribune*, accessed May 16, 2022, at http://tribune.com.pk/story/992728/anticipating-effects-cpec-to-cause-enemplymentingilgitbaltistan/

77 Ibid

78 Ibid

79 Daily Bang-e-Sahar (2015), "CPEC Will Benefit Punjab and Gilgit-Baltistan Will Only Get Labour and Dust," accessed May 22, 2022 at www.bangesahar.net/popup.php?r_date=11-30-2015&img=11-30-2015page-1-2

80 According to the Mine and Minerals Department of Gilgit-Baltistan, "Different aspects of National Mineral Policy have been implemented in the provinces to a varying degree but up till now no major break-through has been achieved in the sector primarily due to lack of infrastructure facilities in the mineral bearing areas and high risk nature of investment in the sector. Under the constitutional frame work, Government, of Pakistan is responsible for policy formulation, generation of geological data and exploration targets." The GB region has minerals worth billions of dollars. Around Rs. 500 million values of gemstones are

extracted annually from Gilgit-Baltistan and efforts are underway to explore other precious minerals. It has been confirmed that nearly all valleys in Gilgit-Baltistan have reserves of gold and base metals but the lack of investment and oversight has meant that the region or its people has not benefited. Due to the lack of oversight, it is alleged that a number of foreign companies with the support of corrupt officials have exploited more resources than permitted to the detriment of the local economy. Apart from over mining, the region also faces the problem of illegal mining, which has a long history in Pakistan and has played an increasing role as a source of rural employment and revenue. The absence of an effective regulatory state, as well as failure to develop a longterm strategy to harness labour force potential, has led to its growth. The fact that this region has uranium deposits and the possibility of illegal smuggling of this mineral is worrisome The role of Chinese mining companies extracting uranium without any restriction or regulation of the federal or local government has been accused by the locals. For more, see, Dhrubajyoti Bhattacharya (2019), *"Exploitation of Water and Mineral Resources of Gilgit-Baltistan,"* ICW, accessed July 28, 2022 https://www.icwa.in/show_content.php?lang=1&level=1&ls_id=2726&lid=2022

CONCLUSION

With the decline in the political situation in Jammu and Kashmir, especially since the 1990s, occasioned primarily by Pakistani strategy of subversion and terrorism, there was a general perception among the people that the state has been a victim of governance deficit, central interference and massive corruption, which have led to overall developmental deficit and decline in human capital. The case of Indian highhandedness and overbearing control through deployment of a large number of security forces has been pushed through hyper-propaganda spread by the hostile media in Pakistan and some unfriendly media houses at the international level over the last four decades to this effect. Such criticism does not, however, take into account the context which has dictated the Indian response. It does not also make any comparative assessment of the measures taken by India and many other countries at the international level to deal with similar challenges. That India's hand has been forced through clever manipulation of the political dynamics within a sensitive state bordering Pakistan is often lost sight of. Those disregarding the unremitting Pakistani gameplan to use terror as an instrument of its policy towards India usually overlook the fact that despite the compulsions that India has, to safeguard its territorial frontiers, it has adopted a much more benign policy than any other state confronted with secession and separatist assertion.

There has been a steady and incessant campaign by Pakistan against India with effective use of the media and diplomacy, which has corrupted the imagination of impressionable minds in J&K and raised an architecture of violence, which some have called the 'terror industry'. Every response of the security force to violence and provocation is tweaked, overexaggerated and presented in a manner that portrays India as a predatory state eternally conspiring against the Kashmiris with an overtly communal outlook. The innocent people of Kashmir have, quite easily, fallen victim to such propaganda and believed in the twisted facts served to them with bad intent. This has not only alienated the people from India but also deepened the divide between India and J&K. The people have chosen to turn a blind eye to the happenings within Pakistan, a victim of the violence they have themselves raised so carefully over the years. They have forgotten how in the name of Islam, Pakistanis are killing each other and how different ethnic communities, especially the minority ones, are being discriminated against and suffering at the hands of a militarized state. They are not aware of the fact that the deep state of Pakistan, which weaves this web of lies and deceit, is doing it all to keep hostility with India in tact, wherefrom they draw their sustenance in Pakistani politics and power structure. The political leadership of J&K, both in the mainstream and at the peripheries (the separatists) has chosen to take full advantage of the situation and added to the muddle rather than making any real attempt to build bridges between the people of Kashmir and rest of India. Rather than working for and with India, they have succumbed to the Pakistani machinations out of fear and sustained the atmosphere of distrust worsening the situation in Kashmir with every passing year. The separate status accorded to J&K by the Indian state in 1950 was used by them as a shield against any constructive intervention by India to change the political dynamic in Kashmir. They told lies to the people and shed crocodile's tears over their condition, while they contributed to the crisis in a big way. With the constitutional measures taken by the Indian state, out of deep frustration with the locus of development in J&K, the situation at present is ripe for innovative and constructive politics and it is incumbent on the people to choose dynamic and honest leaders who can lead them out of the current state of alienation and estrangement from India.

The people of J&K are also not too aware of the way Pakistan has treated the twin regions within PoJK. The people living there do not have political rights and their resources are being plundered mindlessly by Pakistan against their wishes. They have suffered heavily under both democratic and dictatorial rules from Islamabad. A small ministry at Islamabad, known as the ministry for KANA (Kashmir and Norther Areas) affairs used to rule PoJK for years and is still responsible for governance in both 'AJK' and 'GB'. What is worse, the terror infrastructure that targets J&K has been raised in these areas making the people vulnerable to Indian attacks on one side and subjected them to international criticism on the other. Pakistan's developmental inverstment has been minimal even if the region has tremendous tourism and economic potential. Those living in PoJK are treated almost like 'stateless', 'unrepresented' people with nominal rights.

The data collected and analysed in the earlier chapters negate the hypothesis advanced by advocates of violence and resistance in J&K that the state has been at the receiving end as far as Indian economic and developmental policies are concerned. The data indicate that over the last 75 years, the state of Jammu and Kashmir in India has had a better developmental profile than the area under illegal occupation of Pakistan known as PoJK. There is a clear lag as far as PoJK is concerned in most indices of development ranging from the very basic ones like life expectancy and literacy to healthcare and education. Moreover, the control of Pakistan over the resources of PoJK is immense, but the people of PoJK are bereft of the benefits of resources. They organise regular protests on many occasions and have made their discontent for Pakistan felt in the occupied region. There are no democratic rights for the people in PoJK.

In comparison, in Jammu and Kashmir, people exercise their democratic rights and have been given the freedom to choose their own leaders. J&K-based political parties continue to have good presence in local politics, unlike the case in Pakistan where local parties have nearly vanished. Pakistan has been trying everything to absorb PoJK undet the claim of Kashmir benega Pakistan on the basis of the outmoded 'Two Nation Theory', that forms the ideological foundation of Pakistan. Kashmir is projected by Pakistan as the jugular vein, a vital part of its identity. It continues to perceive itself as an incomplete Muslim state denied of strategic depth without the accession of Kashmir to Pakistan, which imagines itself as a Muslim mother state encompassing all adjacent areas with Muslim majority like the state of Jammu and Kashmir. To achieve that goal, the Pakistan state has created, sponsored and allied itself with a menagerie of violent non-state actors.

India has projected Kashmir a symbol of its secular nationalism, and has tried its best to protect J&K from terrorism, exported from Pakistan. Knowling fully well that Pakistan has managed to corrupt the minds of the people of Kashmir, it has adopted a policy of minimum control and interference even in the face of grave provocations, and sought to bring reason to the people through non-kinetic means and avert bloodshed. While falling into the traps of Pakistani propaganda, the people of J&K overlook the Pakistani strategy of use-of-maximum-force while dealing with separatist forces in the country. The cases of villages being razed to ground and attacked by helicopter gun-ships, disappearances of rebels everyday by state forces and non-state actors funded by the state are not known or discussed in the valley. That Pakistan has been hell-bent, right from the beginning, on incorporating Kashmir into its territory by all means is lost on the people of Kashmir. The facts gathered in the book indicate that in the absence of Pakistan-sponsored terrorism, J&K would be the crowning glory of the Indian state as an example of unity and amity. It is time that in light of findings in this volume, the people of J&K take a fresh and positive look at India, which has been quite firm in its commitment to use democratic principles to bring peace and prosperity to J&K.

BIBLIOGRAPHY

AG Noorani, *The Kashmir Dispute: 1947-2012 (2 volumes)*, Tulika Books: New Delhi, 2017

Ahmad Hasan Dani, *History of the Northern Areas of Pakistan*, Sang-e-Meel Publications: Krachi, 2001.

Ajaz Ashraf Wani, *What Happened to Governance in Kashmir?*, Oxford University Press: New Delhi, 2018.

Altaf Hussain, *The Gilgit Baltistan Reforms 2009*, Report by the Forum of Federations Project, December 2009.

Alastair Lamb, *Kashmir: A Disputed Legacy (1846-1990)*, Roxford Books: Hertfordshire, 1991.

Amar Singh Chohan, *Gilgit Agency 1877–1935*, Atlantic Publishers: New Delhi, 1997.

Ashish Shukla, *Gilgit-Baltistan under Pakistan's Occupation'*, Indian Council of World Affairs: New Delhi, 2021.

C. Christine Fair, *In Their Own Words: Understanding Lashkar-e-Tayyaba*, Oxford University Press, New Delhi, 2019.

Chitralekha Zutshi, *Kashmir's Contested Pasts: Narratives, Sacred Geographies and the Historical Imagination*, Oxford University Press: New Delhi, 2014.

Christopher Snedden, *The Untold Story of the People of Azad Kashmir*, Oxford University Press: UK, 2011.

Christopher Snedden, *Understanding Kashmir and Kashmiris*, Hearst: London, 2015.

Iqbal Chand Malhotra and Maroof Raza (2019), *Kashmir's Untold Story*, Bloomsbury: India.

Jasjit Singh (ed.), *Pakistan Occupied Kashmir: Under the Jackboot*, Cosmo Publications: New Delhi.

Luv Puri, *Across the Line of Control. Inside Azad Kashmir*, Columbia University Press, 2010.

Muhammad Amir Rana and Mujtaba Rathore, *Northern Areas: Crisis and Prospects, Pakistan Institute for Peace Studies*, Lahore, 2007.

Navneeta Chadha Behera, *State, Identity and Violence: Jammu, Kashmir and Ladakh*, Manohar Publishers: New Delhi, 2000.

Navneeta Chadha Behera, *Demystifying Kashmir*, Pearson Longman: USA, 2007.

Praveen Swami, *India, Pakistan and the Secret Jihad: The Covert War in Kashmir, 1947-2004,* Routledge: New Delhi, 2006.

Rekha Chowdhary, *Jammu and Kashmir: 1990 and Beyond: Competitive Politics in the Shadow of Separatism*, Sage: New Delhi, 2019.

Shabir Choudhry, *Tribal Invasion and Kashmir: Pakistani Attempts to Capture Kashmir in 1947, Division of Kashmir and Terrorism*, Bloomington: Author House, 2013.

Sisir Gupta, *Kashmir: A Study in India-Pakistan Relations,* Asia Publishing House: New Delhi, 1966.

Sumit Ganguly, *The Kashmir question: retrospect and prospect,* Frank Cass: London, 2003.

Surinder Kumar Sharma, Yaqoob ul Hassan and Ashok Behuria, *Pakistan Occupied Kashmir: Politics, Parties and Personalities*, Pentagon Press LLP: New Delhi, 2019.

Victoria Schofield, *Kashmir in Conflict: India, Pakistan and the Unending War,* I.B Tauris: London and New York, 2003.

Virendra Gupta and Alok Bansal (eds.), *Pakistan Occupied Kashmir: The Untold Story*, Manas Publications: New Delhi, 2007.

ABBREVIATIONS

AJK	Azad Jammu and Kashmir
AJKMC	Azad Jammu and Kashmir Muslim Conference
CAGR	Compund Annual Growth Rate
CoK	China Occupied Kashmir
CPEC	China Pakistan Economic Corridor
FCNA	Force Commander Northern Areas
GB	Gilgit Baltistan
GBC	Gilgit-Baltistan Council
GBCCI	Gilgit Baltistan, Chamber of Commerce
GBLA	Gilgit Baltistan Legislative Assembly
GBESGO	Gilgit-Baltistan Empowerment and Self-Governance Order
FCR	Frontier Crimes Regulations
HRCP	Human Rights Commission Pakistan
ISI	Inter-Services Intelligence
ICG	International Crisis Group

J&K	Jammu and Kashmir
JKLL	Jammu and Kashmir Liberation League
KAGB	Kashmir Affairs and Gilgit Baltistan
KANA	Kashmir and Northern Areas
LeT	Lashkar-e-Toiba
LoC	Line of Control
MKA	Ministry of Kashmir Affairs
MKANA	Ministry of Kashmir Affairs and Northern Areas
NFC	National Finance Commission
NSSO	National Sample Survey Office
NWFP	North-West Frontier Province
PML-N	Pakistan Muslim League-Nawaz
PoJK	Pakistan occupied Jammu Kashmir
PPP	Pakistan People's Party
PTI	Pakistan Tehreek-i-Insaf
TFR	Total Fertility Rate
UNCIP	United Nations Commission for India and Pakistan

LIST OF TABLES

MAPS

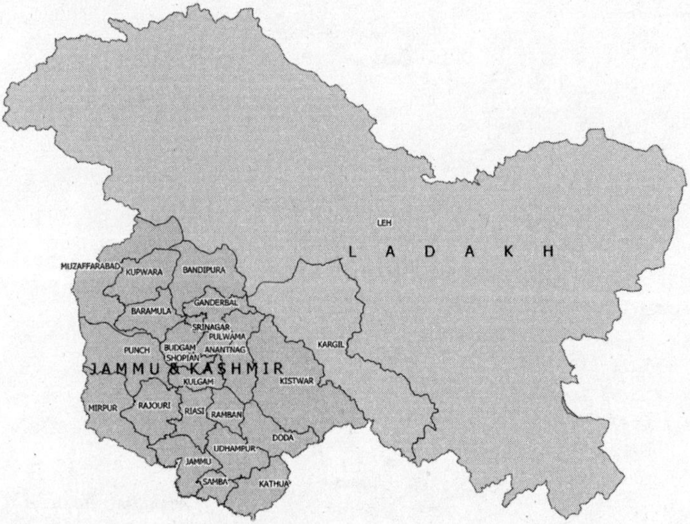

Map of UT of Jammu and Kashmir and UT of Ladakh.
Source: https://static.pib.gov.in/WriteReadData/userfiles/Map%20of%20UTs.pdf

Administrative Boundary of UT Jammu and Kashmir.
Source: https://static.pib.gov.in/WriteReadData/userfiles/UT%20of%20J&K.pdf

UN Map of Jammu and Kashmir Area Showing the Line of Control.

Source: https://www.un.org/geospatial/file/2006/download?token=H9q3B2Zx

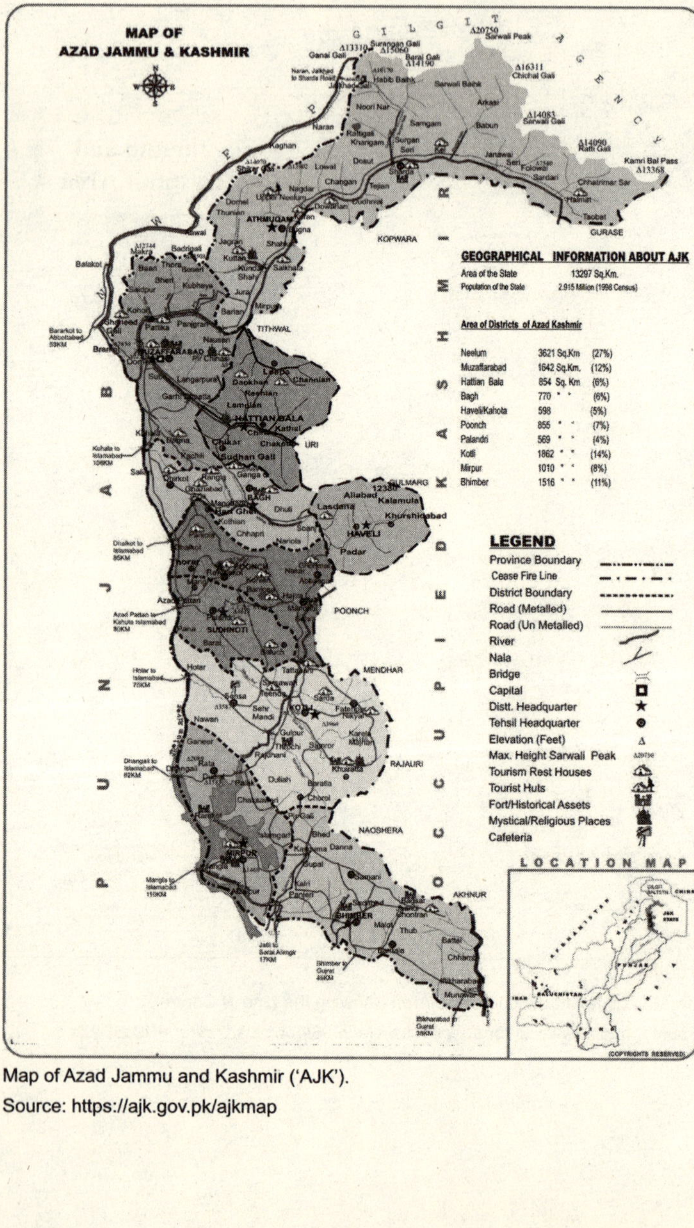

Map of Azad Jammu and Kashmir ('AJK').

Source: https://ajk.gov.pk/ajkmap

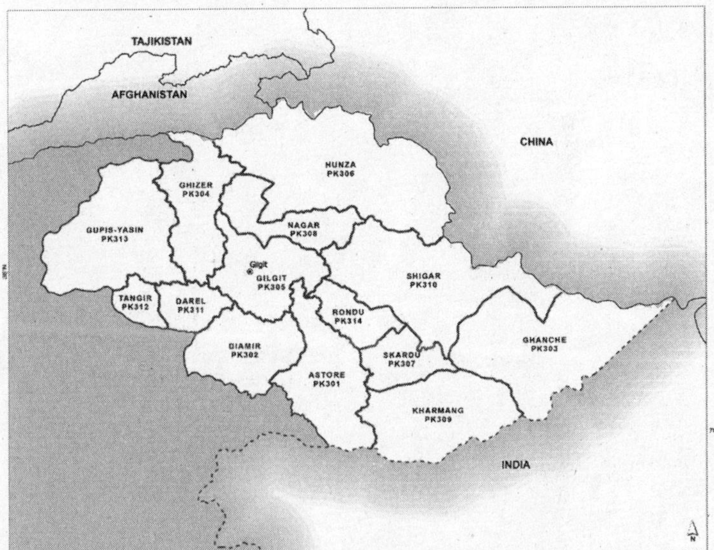

Administrative Map of Gilgit-Baltistan.

Source: https://reliefweb.int/attachments/bb098171-a116-400e-a2c7-69934259b305/ma005-v02-pak-provinces_districts_mapseries-300dpi.pdf

OTHER BOOKS BY THE AUTHOR